Evil Sister

What will Victoria do? Savannah wondered as she rushed to the slave quarters. She knew that was where Victoria would go.

She must be furious. I know she wanted Tyler for herself. I have to make her understand we didn't mean to hurt her.

But what if I can't? What if she refuses to listen?

A cold chill ran through Savannah's body. What will she do? What will Victoria try to do to us?

As she neared the slave quarters, she heard a terrified squeal coming from one of the old shacks.

She quickened her pace. Oh, Victoria, Savannah thought. What have you done?

The squealing grew louder.

With her heart pounding, Savannah opened the door and peered inside the shack.

She pressed her hands against her lips, trying to muffle a gasp.

Victoria stood in the center of the shadowy room.

Streaks of bright r̶ face.

FEAR STREET SAGAS® #3
R.L. STINE

Forbidden Secrets

A Parachute Press Book

AN ARCHWAY PAPERBACK
Published by POCKET BOOKS
New York London Toronto Sydney Tokyo Singapore

AN ARCHWAY PAPERBACK *Original*

An Archway Paperback published by
POCKET BOOKS, a division of Simon & Schuster Inc.
1230 Avenue of the Americas, New York, NY 10020

Copyright © 1996 by Parachute Press, Inc.

FORBIDDEN SECRETS WRITTEN BY BRANDON ALEXANDER

ISBN: 0-671-52954-4

First Archway Paperback printing September 1996

10 9 8 7 6 5 4 3 2 1

FEAR STREET is a registered trademark of
Parachute Press, Inc.

AN ARCHWAY PAPERBACK and colophon are
registered trademarks of Simon & Schuster Inc.

Cover art by Lisa Falkenstern

Printed in the U.S.A.

IL 7+

Forbidden Secrets

Blackrose Manor

The black roses were in bloom.

Their scent hung heavy in the air. So sweet, so sickly sweet.

The withered old woman drew her black shawl over her narrow, stooped shoulders. The roses surrounded her as she sat in her garden.

Their presence chilled her to the bone.

I long for the sweet scent of magnolias, the woman thought. She clutched her shawl with her gnarled hands. I long for the home of my youth.

Whispering Oaks.

She closed her eyes.

I often dream of returning. But more than distance keeps me away.

It is also the passage of time.

And betrayal.

The old woman opened her eyes and gazed at the

black roses. She imagined that she could see her reflection in the glistening dewdrops on the petals.

"I have grown old here at Blackrose Manor," she murmured. "I have grown old dreaming of Whispering Oaks."

Too many years have passed since I was last at the family plantation, she thought. And yet the memories do not fade. They remain strong. They haunt me.

Perhaps it is time I spoke of the past. Perhaps it is time I told the story . . . told the secrets. Perhaps if I do, I will again be able to sleep at night.

But whom could I tell? Who would care enough to listen to my tale of woe?

I should tell the story to my sister. I have not spoken to her in years. And she is so close. So close.

She sleeps next to me . . . deep inside her dark grave.

The black roses grow over her resting place. They serve as her blanket. But it must be cold in her bed— as cold as my heart.

My sister would not listen to me when she lived.

Perhaps she will listen to me now.

My story begins long ago . . . when I was young. Before my hands grew stiff and twisted. Before my skin became wrinkled and my hair white.

My story is the tale of two sisters, Victoria and Savannah . . . two doomed sisters.

We grew up together on our father's plantation, Whispering Oaks.

Savannah was the beautiful sister. Everyone said so. Her hair was the blond of moonbeams. Her eyes were the green of spring.

From the moment she was born, she was the

favorite. Our mother pampered her and our father spoiled her.

Victoria was the smart sister. Everyone called her that. Or, if people were unkind, the odd sister. She did not have Savannah's beauty. Her hair and eyes were as brown as the soil in the cotton fields.

Life was peaceful for the sisters. Perhaps it would have remained so were it not for the events of the spring of 1861.

That was the spring our brother, Zachariah, returned home from West Point. He brought a friend with him—a young cadet.

Tyler Fier.

How different our lives would have been if Zachariah had not brought his friend to the plantation.

Tyler was the handsomest man I had ever seen. His hair was as black as the night sky when there is no moon. And his eyes were as blue as a lake in winter.

I fell in love with him the moment I saw him.

As did my sister.

Perhaps if she had not fallen in love with him, we would not be here now.

Perhaps if I had not fallen in love with him, my story would have a happier ending.

I can hear the voices from the past circling around me now. They surround me just as the roses do.

The old woman trailed her finger along the velvet edge of a black rose petal.

Then she pricked herself on a thorn.

Blood trickled down her finger.

Black blood.

Drop by drop it dripped from her finger and soaked into the ground.

PART ONE

Whispering Oaks
Georgia,
Spring 1861

Chapter
1

Savannah Gentry stood on the wide balcony of Whispering Oaks, her family's magnificent plantation house.

She gazed out over her father's land. On any other day, she would have seen slaves toiling in the distant fields. The cotton they planted and picked made her father a wealthy man.

But the slaves were not working in the fields today. This was a special day, a day of celebration.

The older slaves set the tables for Savannah's party. The younger slaves turned spitted calves and pigs over blazing open fires.

Neighbors from miles around had been invited to share this momentous day—as her father called it. The day of Savannah's birth.

Even her brother, Zachariah, had returned from West Point in time to attend her birthday party. And he brought a friend along.

Tyler Fier.

Savannah smiled when she thought of Tyler. I have known him less than two weeks, she realized. But already I feel that he is a part of me.

I should never have let him out of my sight this morning. Savannah stomped her foot.

I shall give Zachariah a proper tongue-lashing when he returns from his ride with Tyler, she decided. My brother knows Tyler will soon leave for his home in the North. It was selfish of him to take Tyler riding without me.

She stood on tiptoe. Straining to see any sign of the two young men.

"Fiddle!" She dropped her heels back on the floor and smoothed the skirt of her green silk gown. "They promised to be back in time for the picnic."

Savannah heard the rumble of wagon wheels. She walked to the corner of the balcony and peered around the corner at the front of the estate.

Wagons filled with laughing couples traveled up the dirt path. Savannah barely glanced at the young men driving the wagons. Once she had taken an interest in those young men. Once she had sat beneath the shade of an oak tree and sipped lemonade with each of them. And once she had promised to marry each and every one of them.

Now she cared only about Tyler.

"Fiddle!" she repeated. "I wanted him here to meet my friends."

Then she heard the sound of pounding hooves. She whirled back to face the fields. Tyler galloped toward the plantation house on his black horse, Zachariah close behind.

Lifting her green hoopskirt, Savannah rushed into her bedroom. She snatched up her matching green parasol. Then she raced out of her room and down the sweeping stairs into the grand entryway.

"Savannah!"

She skidded to a stop at the sound of her mother's voice.

Her mother walked gracefully across the foyer. "Ladies do not run," she scolded. "Especially young ladies who have just turned seventeen."

Savannah blushed. "I know, Mother, but Tyler is waiting for me."

Her mother smiled gently. "Tyler, Tyler, Tyler. Every sentence you utter these days has his name in it."

"I enjoy his company," Savannah said breathlessly.

"Have you seen your sister?" her mother asked. "Have you seen Victoria this afternoon?"

"No," Savannah answered. "But I am sure she will be at the picnic."

Her mother's eyes grew troubled. "I hope so. I hope she is not in the slave quarters again." She shook her head. "I do not approve of the strange habits she is acquiring."

Savannah shuddered. She didn't like the changes in Victoria either. And she knew something her mother didn't. Victoria was fascinated by the dark arts some of the slave women practiced.

Victoria wanted their strange powers for herself. That was the true reason she spent so much time in the slave quarters.

I won't worry about Victoria now, Savannah decided. I won't let my sister spoil my birthday.

Chapter
2

"See you at the picnic, Mama," Savannah called as she rushed out the wide front doors.

Zachariah and Tyler walked over as soon as she set foot on the porch.

"I would like to show your sister one of the flowers in the garden. I have never seen it growing in the North—and I thought she could tell me its name," Tyler said.

Please, Zach, Savannah begged silently. Please, oh, please. She could count on one hand the number of times she and Tyler had managed to be alone.

Zachariah winked at her, his green eyes sparkling. "I wouldn't want to stop you from studying our beautiful southern flowers," he told his friend. "But don't take too long—or I'll have to come looking for you."

Savannah felt herself blushing as Tyler led her down

the porch steps, across the formal gardens, and deep into the woods.

"I stumbled across this spot on a walk," Tyler said when the trees gave way to a clearing. Now Savannah could see the small white gazebo sitting next to the lake.

"Zach used to take girls here," Savannah admitted.

Tyler broke a magnolia blossom off a tree. He handed it to her as they stepped inside the wooden gazebo.

"I love the fragrance of magnolias," she said.

Tyler wrapped his arms around her waist and drew her close. Our first kiss, Savannah thought as he lowered his lips to hers.

I can't breathe Savannah thought wildly. I can't breathe and I do not care. She loved the feel of his arms around her, the warmth of his mouth over hers.

Finally, Savannah broke away from the kiss. Gasping for air, she pressed her cheek against his chest. She heard his heart pounding as rapidly as hers. "I will never survive when you leave!"

He tightened his arms around her. "Come with me."

She jerked her head back and looked into his eyes.

"Marry me, Savannah." He did not wait for her answer. Eagerly, he kissed her again.

And with her kiss, Savannah gave him her answer. Yes! Yes! Yes!

A sudden cold breeze rustled the leaves of the nearby trees. Savannah felt the hair on the nape of her neck rise.

A strange feeling swept through her. We're being

watched, she realized with alarm. *I can feel someone watching us.*

She pulled away from Tyler and quickly glanced around. But she didn't see anyone. "I'm sorry. I thought someone was watching us," Savannah explained.

Tyler's blue eyes darkened. "And what would they see?"

She smiled softly and wrapped her arms around him. "Two people who plan to spend the rest of their lives together."

He brushed his lips over her forehead, the tip of her nose, and her cheek. "I want to announce our engagement today! At the picnic!"

A twig snapped. Savannah jumped away from Tyler and spun around.

"Someone *is* watching us!" she cried.

Tyler slipped his arms around her and kissed her shoulder. "It's just a squirrel," he said.

"No," Savannah insisted. Savannah scanned the edge of the clearing. Her green eyes narrowed.

"There!" she cried. She pointed her finger at someone half hidden by the trees.

Her sister! Victoria with her brown eyes and her brown hair. Victoria, whose coloring blended in with the bark of the trees.

Her sister darted away.

"Victoria!" Savannah called. *"Victoria!"*

"Let her go," Tyler said.

Savannah turned and faced him. "I can't. Our engagement will be hard on her. Victoria hoped you would take an interest in her—"

"What?" Tyler exclaimed.

"You did meet her first. And you were very flattering," Savannah reminded him.

"Polite. I was polite," Tyler protested. He pulled her back into his arms and kissed her again.

Savannah loved the feel of Tyler's lips on hers. But finally she forced herself to pull away. "I know you meant only to be polite, but please understand. I must talk with her before we make our announcement."

He kissed her lightly. "Very well. Go on. I will wait for you out by the tables."

What will Victoria do? Savannah wondered as she rushed to the slave quarters. She knew that was where Victoria would go.

She must be furious. I know she wanted Tyler for herself. I have to make her understand we didn't mean to hurt her.

But what if I can't? Savannah thought. What if she refuses to listen?

A cold chill ran through Savannah's body. What will she do? What will Victoria try to do to us?

As she neared the slave quarters, she heard a terrified squeal coming from one of the old shacks.

She quickened her pace. Oh, Victoria, Savannah thought. What have you done?

The squealing grew louder.

With her heart pounding, Savannah opened the door and peered inside the shack.

She pressed her hands against her lips, trying to muffle a gasp.

Victoria stood in the center of the shadowy room.

Streaks of bright red blood ran down her face.

Chapter
3

Savannah stared at her sister. She couldn't speak.

Victoria was holding a pink piglet in the center of a large wooden table. Flickering candles formed a half circle around the piglet. The flames danced wildly as it squealed.

The odor of scorched flesh and singed hair filled Savannah's nostrils. She could see the orange flames in the hearth licking greedily at the remains of another piglet.

Tremors shook Savannah's body as she watched her sister.

Victoria dipped her hand into a silver bowl. When she lifted her hand from the bowl, bright red blood—fresh blood—flowed from her cupped palm. She sprinkled the blood over one of the candles. The flame hissed, sputtered, and died.

Victoria repeated the ritual with each candle until all the flames were extinguished. Thin trails of black smoke spiraled toward the ceiling. The piglet kicked its legs and squealed frantically.

How can she do this evil thing? Savannah thought.

Victoria began to sway from side to side. *"Dominatio per malum.* Fire. Fear. Betrayal. Revenge," she chanted.

Terror surged through Savannah. What do those words mean? she asked herself. Does Victoria think that I betrayed her? Is she planning revenge?

No, Victoria would never harm me, Savannah told herself. But why is she doing this?

Victoria picked up a large knife. She lifted it high into the air. She threw her head back. "I do this for you, Savannah!" she cried.

"Victoria, no!" Savannah yelled as she rushed toward her sister.

She shoved Victoria away from the table. The knife clattered to the floor. The piglet scrambled to its feet. Savannah lifted it off the table and it scurried out of the shack.

Victoria continued to sway, repeating the words in a hoarse voice. "Fear. Betrayal. Revenge."

She doesn't realize I stopped her, Savannah thought with alarm. She doesn't even know I'm here!

"Victoria!" Savannah cried.

Victoria ignored her. Her brown eyes glazed over.

She is in a trance, Savannah realized, her heart pounding.

Savannah grabbed Victoria and gasped. My sister is as cold as ice, she thought. I can feel the cold seeping through her clothes.

Savannah dug her fingers into Victoria's shoulders and shook her. "Victoria! Victoria, what is wrong with you?"

Victoria began to moan. Tears flowed down her cheeks.

"Forgive me, Victoria," Savannah whispered. She slapped her sister's bloodstained face.

Victoria's head snapped to the side. Savannah's hand stung. She gave her sister another shake. "Victoria!"

Victoria blinked. Once. Twice. Then she shuddered. The light of awareness returned to her eyes. "Savannah!"

Savannah sighed with relief. She sees me, Savannah thought. Victoria snapped out of the trance.

Then Savannah grew angry. "What are you doing in here?" she demanded.

Fear showed in Victoria's eyes as she stared around the shack. "Where is Tyler?"

"At the party. I came here because I wanted to talk to you."

Victoria narrowed her brown eyes. "I don't trust Tyler."

"Did you think you could hurt him by killing little pigs?" Savannah asked.

"I thought I could learn something about him through performing this ritual." Victoria smiled triumphantly. "And I did."

Savannah fumed. "You have no right—"

"I have every right," Victoria insisted in a rush. "I'm older than you are. I have to protect you."

"I don't need you to protect me from Tyler." Savannah spun on her heel and began to walk away.

"You're wrong!" Victoria cried. "Tyler Fier comes from a cursed family."

Savannah whipped around and glared at her sister. "That's ridiculous. I love Tyler. I know him as well as I know myself. This"—she pointed toward the bloody table—"is nothing more than a cruel game. I don't believe in the dark arts."

Victoria took a step forward. "You should believe, Savannah. The dark arts revealed the truth to me. Evil stalks the Fier family."

Savannah sighed wearily. "Victoria, I know you hoped to marry Tyler. I know you overheard Tyler asking me to marry him. I know you're disappointed. But nothing you say will stop me from marrying Tyler."

"You don't understand!" Victoria wailed. She wrapped her arms around herself and sank to the floor. Then she rocked back and forth, back and forth, over and over. "You don't understand!"

Savannah dropped down beside her sister. "I do understand. You feel hurt—"

"No!" Victoria cried shrilly. "You are the one who will be hurt. I'm trying to protect you! Madness. Death. Hatred. They all follow the Fier family. And they will follow you if you don't break off your relationship—"

Savannah held up her hand to stop her sister's

ranting. "You are jealous, Victoria. Jealous because you met Tyler first—and he chose your little sister over you."

"That's not true," Victoria insisted. She grabbed Savannah's hands. Her fingernails dug into Savannah's palms. "I'm worried about *you*. You must stay away from Tyler Fier!"

Chapter
4

"I can't stay away from Tyler," Savannah said quietly as she rose to her feet. "I love him."

"He will bring you nothing but unhappiness," Victoria warned her.

"The only one bringing me unhappiness is you," Savannah said sadly. She took Victoria's hands and helped her stand. "You are my sister, Victoria, and I love you very much. I want you to share the happiest day of my life with me."

"I don't want you to get hurt," Victoria mumbled.

"Then come back to the picnic with me."

Victoria nodded. Savannah led her sister to a nearby bucket of water.

I wish Tyler had not been so polite when he first met Victoria, Savannah thought as she gently washed the blood off her sister's face. But how was he to know that Victoria would fall in love with him so quickly? Or that he would fall in love with me?

When Victoria was clean, Savannah slipped her arm around her sister's waist. In silence, they walked away from the slave quarters. They strolled across the formal grounds. As they neared the plantation house, Savannah saw Tyler leaning against a tree, watching her.

Will he always make my heart beat so fast? she wondered. Will the sight of him always steal my breath away?

Tyler sauntered toward them. "I want to make your sister happy," he told Victoria firmly.

"Then leave her." Victoria walked away without another word.

Savannah placed her hand on Tyler's arm. "Ignore her. She's jealous. She wanted you, but you wanted me."

Savannah's heart fluttered at the intensity of his dark blue eyes.

"Forever, Savannah," Tyler said in a low voice. "You will be mine forever."

"Forever," she vowed, and joy swelled within her heart.

A far-off shout made Savannah spin around. She saw a horse galloping along the dirt path. The rider frantically waved a newspaper in the air. "War!" he shouted. "War has broken out!"

The man pulled his horse to a halt as people rushed to gather around him. "Fort Sumter has been fired upon!" he yelled so all could hear him. "We are at war!"

"War," Savannah whispered hoarsely. War! her heart screamed. Tyler is now a soldier, she realized with sickening dread. And soldiers die!

Savannah pressed her cheek against Tyler's chest. "Please don't go," she whispered.

He gathered her within his arms. "I must go, Savannah," he said quietly.

"What if you are killed?" she asked, her voice quivering.

He laughed. "I won't be killed. Not if I have you waiting for me." He put his hands on her shoulders and gently pushed her back. He gazed into her green eyes. "You will wait, won't you?"

"Of course I'll wait. And with you fighting beside Zachariah—"

"Beside Zachariah?" he interrupted in a stunned voice. "I won't fight beside Zachariah. I will fight for the North."

Bewildered, Savannah tried to understand exactly what he was telling her. "The North? You can't possibly fight for the North!"

"I can and I will," he said in a low, calm voice.

Savannah wrenched free of Tyler's hold and stepped away from him. With one word—war!— Tyler has become my enemy, she realized sadly. He will fight to destroy the South, my home, my family.

Savannah trembled. Hot tears stung her eyes. "Fight for the South, Tyler," she begged in desperation. "Fight for my home and my family."

"I must fight for *my* home, Savannah. My loyalty is to the North!"

"And what of your loyalty to *me?*" she demanded angrily.

22

His features hardened. "I'll marry you today. I'll take you to my home in Massachusetts. Then you and my home will be in the North. My loyalty won't be divided."

"No. I can't marry you," Savannah said. "Not now."

"You will marry me!" he insisted.

Savannah stood her ground. She threw back her shoulders and lifted her chin in defiance. "If I marry you, I'll have to turn my back on the South. I won't do that."

His face turned red with rage. "I asked you to marry me, Savannah," he whispered. "You said yes!"

"That was before I knew the truth about you!" she cried. "That was before I knew you would fight for the North. I cannot love someone who will fight to destroy my home and my family. I will *not* love you!"

He balled his hands into fists. "You have no choice. You are already mine!"

"No!" she replied. "If you fight for the North, I won't love you. I will never marry you."

Fierce anger glinted in his eyes. A cold shiver raced down Savannah's spine.

"I am leaving to fight with the northern army," he said through gritted teeth. "Come with me now."

"Never!" Savannah repeated, her heart thudding in her chest. "You are a traitor to my home, my brother's friendship, and our love. I will never marry you!"

Tears blinding her, Savannah ran to the house. She collapsed against one of the marble pillars.

The pain of Tyler's betrayal ripped through her.

How can Tyler fight for the North when I live in the

South? How could he be my love one moment and my enemy the next?

And then she heard the laughter. Victoria's gleeful laughter. Hysterical. Joyful.

"He's leaving, isn't he?" Victoria asked.

Savannah looked up. She saw Tyler riding his black horse down the dirt road, away from Whispering Oaks, away from her.

And her heart shattered into tiny pieces.

Victoria clapped with delight.

She is happy that he is going, Savannah realized. Incredibly happy. Her jealousy is so apparent. She can't have Tyler, and now she knows I won't have him either.

Savannah saw Tyler bring his horse to an abrupt halt. He jerked the stallion around. He galloped back toward the house. Dust clouded up around him.

He's coming back, Savannah thought joyfully. He's coming back to me! He will take me in his arms and everything will be all right.

Tyler drew the horse to a halt before her. The stallion's black coat was wet and shiny. Savannah could smell the animal's sweat, feel its warm breath as it struggled for air.

Savannah stepped forward and lifted her gaze to Tyler's. His blue eyes still seethed with anger. His handsome face was twisted with fury and hatred.

Tyler reared his horse up so it pranced on its hind legs.

Savannah stumbled back and wrapped her arms around the white marble pillar.

"Mark my words, Savannah Gentry!" Tyler threatened. "I am a man who keeps his promises!"

His horse's hooves hit the ground. Tyler leaned over until his face was even with Savannah's. Icy dread clamped around her heart.

"You will regret choosing the South over me!" Tyler snarled. "I swear it!"

Blackrose Manor

The old woman shuddered at the memory.

So vivid. As though it had all happened yesterday.

She could still hear Tyler's words echoing over the plantation. She could still see Tyler galloping down the dirt road, away from Whispering Oaks.

With a gnarled finger she plucked a rose from a nearby bush. She ripped off a black petal and tossed it into the air. She watched as it floated slowly to the ground.

"Savannah loved him," she said in a raspy voice.

She tugged another petal free and dropped it. It drifted down and settled near her feet.

"Savannah loved him not."

She plucked another petal.

"Savannah loved him."

And another petal.

"Savannah loved him not."

Over and over the old woman plucked a petal and repeated the words.

Finally, all but one of the rose petals lay scattered on the ground.

The old woman held the last petal in her hand and studied it.

"Savannah loved him." She cackled. "No matter how many roses I pick, no matter how many petals I pluck, the last petal always reveals the truth— Savannah loved Tyler Fier."

She wrapped her arms around herself, but she could not ward off the chill in the air. She could not protect herself from the truth. She could not stop herself from remembering.

Everyone knew Savannah's heart broke when Tyler rode away to fight with the Union Army.

But during a war many things broke, the old woman thought. Many things changed.

"Our father's cotton fields became battlefields," the old woman remembered wistfully. "The slaves ran north to freedom. Our parents died."

Wearing a soft smile, the old woman gazed at her sister's grave. "We had only each other," she whispered in a voice that sounded like sandpaper on wood. "Savannah and Victoria. We were left alone at Whispering Oaks.

"Do you remember, dear sister, how frightened we were? How hungry? How worried?"

Tears filled the old woman's eyes.

"But we survived, you and I. Together we survived. And we became so close again. The way we were when we were small children. We began to tell each other everything. Our fears. Our hopes. Our dreams. Sometimes you even talked about Tyler."

With a sigh, the old woman closed her eyes, remembering past conversations. Savannah wanted—needed—to talk about Tyler.

And Victoria listened.

Savannah knew that Tyler betrayed her love. But still she feared for him.

Savannah wondered if she would ever see Tyler again.

She wanted to tell Tyler that she still loved him.

She needed to tell Tyler that she loved him.

As the months of the war dragged into years, Savannah's desperation grew.

Chapter
5

Whispering Oaks
Summer 1863

Savannah walked across the old vegetable garden. "I'll look here," she said to Victoria. "You look over there."

We will not go hungry tonight, Savannah promised herself. We won't. She sank down on the warm soil and began searching through the withered cornstalks and blackened tomato plants. I have to find us something to eat.

Savannah glanced over at Victoria. Her sister's dress hung loosely over her body. We both look like scarecrows, Savannah realized. She ran her fingers over her frayed skirt. Our clothes have become rags.

How will we survive until Zachariah returns? Without the slaves, we can't grow cotton. And without cotton we can't earn any money.

A cannon rumbled in the distance, interrupting

Savannah's thoughts. The earth trembled beneath her. Savannah heard Victoria give a startled cry.

Savannah looked over at her sister. Victoria huddled near the ground, her eyes wide and frightened. "It's all right, Victoria," Savannah said gently. "The battle is far away."

"Are you certain?" Victoria asked.

"I'm certain."

Poor Victoria, Savannah thought. The cannons frighten her so. Day after day they pound the earth.

Savannah sat back on her heels. She remembered a time when Victoria comforted her. When Savannah was a little girl, thunder terrified her. She would sneak into her big sister's bed whenever there was a storm.

How strange, Savannah thought. Now I am the one comforting Victoria. Telling her not to be afraid of loud noises.

Savannah dug her fingers into the dirt. Searching for hidden vegetables. But she found nothing. Her stomach rumbled.

I won't be able to protect Victoria from starvation, Savannah thought. Then she shook her head. Do not think the worst, she scolded herself. We will survive. We will!

"Savannah!" Victoria cried. "Savannah, come quickly!"

Savannah jerked her head up. She could see Victoria pulling something from the earth and working feverishly to fill the bowl in front of her.

Food! Savannah realized. At last we will have something to eat!

"Hurry!" Victoria called out.

Savannah struggled to her feet. She hurried across

the garden and knelt down in the dirt beside her sister. Victoria's face was hollow and drawn, but her brown eyes sparkled with excitement.

Savannah peered into the wooden bowl. She saw a rotting potato and two tiny shriveled carrots.

And she saw the worms.

Fat and juicy, they crawled up one side of the potato and rolled down the other side, falling into a squirming heap.

"We'll save the carrots for dessert," Victoria said.

"For dessert?" Savannah asked. Burning bile rose up in her throat. I can't do this, she thought.

Victoria nodded and pulled a worm out of the bowl. The slimy creature dangled between her fingers. She extended it toward Savannah. "You can eat first," Victoria said.

Savannah's stomach ached with hunger. Would you rather eat a worm or starve? she asked herself.

Savannah opened her mouth and dropped her head back. She watched as Victoria's fingers grew nearer. The long, purple worm wiggled and squirmed.

And then it fell.

Fell into Savannah's waiting mouth and slid down her throat.

Chapter
6

That night Savannah snuggled beneath the down-filled comforter. For the first time in weeks, she was not hungry. Victoria and I will survive, Savannah thought as she closed her eyes. We will do what we have to do, eat what we have to eat, and we will survive. Satisfied, she quickly drifted off to sleep.

Bump.

A noise startled her awake.

Savannah struggled to open her eyes. Pale moonlight spilled through the window. What was that sound? she wondered.

Savannah heard the noise again.

Bump.

Thump.

What is it?

Bump.

Thump.

Savannah's heart pounded. She heard footsteps in the hallway. Then something scraped across the floor.

Savannah's mouth went dry. She scrambled out of bed.

Her doorknob rattled—then turned.

Savannah's breath caught in her chest.

The door hinges squealed as the door slowly opened. A tall man stood in the shadowy doorway.

"Who are you?" Savannah demanded, her voice shaking.

The man took a step toward her with his right foot and dragged his left foot behind him.

Step. Drag. Step. Drag.

He turned toward Savannah. The moonlight hit his face.

Savannah's eyes widened with recognition. "Zachariah!"

Gunpowder covered her brother's tattered gray uniform, his face, his hair. The odor burned Savannah's nostrils.

Zachariah's ashen face was grim. His once-vibrant green eyes were dark and vacant. His blond hair matted with sweat and dirt.

And blood!

Savannah's eyes darted to the gaping bullet hole in Zach's head. Dark blood oozed from the wound, glistening in the moonlight.

"Oh, Zachariah! No!" Savannah cried. "You've been hurt!" She reached for her brother. But he stepped away.

"Let me help you," Savannah pleaded.

He shook his head. His lips quivered as he fought to speak. Savannah could see his throat working.

"What is it, Zachariah?" she asked. "What is it you want to tell me?"

He opened his mouth, opened his mouth to speak. And deep red blood spilled from his lips.

Chapter
7

"Zachariah!" Savannah screamed in horror.

Then she woke up, her body trembling and coated with sweat. "It was a dream," she whispered. "I was dreaming."

The door to her room burst open. Savannah shrieked.

Victoria stood in the doorway, her eyes wide with fear. "I heard you scream," Victoria said in a quivering voice.

Savannah held out her arms. "Oh, Victoria!"

Victoria rushed across the room and scrambled onto the bed. Savannah wrapped her arms around her sister.

"I had a nightmare," Savannah told her. She took a deep breath. "I dreamed about Zachariah. He was wounded and he came to tell me something. Something important. He opened his mouth—" She couldn't go on. She couldn't tell Victoria about the blood.

The nightmare was so real, Savannah thought to herself. I could smell the gunpowder and the blood. See Zachariah so clearly. See that horrible wound in his head. Savannah shuddered.

"What did he say?" Victoria demanded.

Savannah hugged her sister tighter. "He didn't say anything. He just disappeared. It was a silly dream."

"Maybe we shouldn't eat worms for supper," Victoria said in a teasing voice.

Savannah giggled, the nightmare fading away. "I think you're right."

"Can I sleep with you?" Victoria asked.

"Yes," Savannah replied, glad for the company. She pulled the blankets over them and watched the shadows play across the ceiling.

"Sissy?" Victoria whispered.

Savannah smiled in the darkness. When Savannah was little, Victoria used to call her that. Savannah had forgotten how much she liked the nickname.

"What?" Savannah asked.

"Do you think this war will ever end?" Victoria asked.

"I'm sure it will," Savannah assured her sister.

"Do you think Zach will come home?"

"Yes," Savannah whispered. But her voice caught.

"I miss Zach," Victoria said.

"I miss him too," Savannah said softly.

"Good night," Victoria murmured. A few minutes later she heard her sister give a gentle snore.

Savannah turned onto her side. She noticed some-

thing on the floor. Something glistening in the moonlight.

She slipped out of bed and knelt on the floor. Her
hand trembled as she touched the shiny, dark drops.

They felt warm.

Savannah raised her hand in front of her. Blood
covered her fingertips. Dark red blood.

Warm blood . . . from the spot where Zachariah
was standing in her dream.

Chapter
8

Savannah got out of bed as soon as it was light. She could not go back to sleep after she discovered the blood on her floor.

Every time she thought about the drops of blood, she felt sick. It must be some strange coincidence, she told herself. Maybe I cut my foot or . . .

Savannah heard a galloping horse. She ran out onto the porch. Timmy, a young boy from a neighboring plantation, rode toward her.

Timmy drew his horse to a halt. "I have a letter for you, Miss Savannah." He handed her an envelope.

Savannah sat down on the porch steps. She stared at the envelope as Timmy rode away. She did not recognize the handwriting.

A shiver ran down her spine. So many letters brought bad news during the war.

Savannah opened the envelope and pulled out the

wrinkled letter. It was spattered with blood. Her heart gave a hard thump when she saw the signature.

Tyler!

Slowly she read the words scrawled across the parchment:

July 1863

Dear Savannah,

Zachariah is dead. I am so sorry. We were both fighting in Gettysburg. I saw him fall. Later I learned of his death.

As I watched the soldiers bury your brother, I imagined myself in the grave beside him—dead. Never seeing you again. Never holding you again.

Forgive me, Savannah. All the deaths in this war made me realize people are more important than North or South.

Wait for me. I will come back for you.

I promise.

Tyler

Savannah clutched the letter to her chest. Tears stung her eyes. Zachariah was dead. And Tyler—

"Sissy! Sissy! What's wrong?" Victoria rushed out onto the porch.

Savannah stared into Victoria's worried face. Savannah opened her mouth, but she could not utter the horrible words—*Zachariah is dead.*

Victoria grabbed the letter. Savannah watched her sister as she read. Victoria gasped and grew pale. Her eyes filled with tears. "No," she whispered.

Savannah pulled Victoria down next to her. She hugged Victoria as her own tears fell.

"Oh, Sissy," Victoria said in a quivering voice. "I can't believe Zach is dead."

"I know. I can't either," Savannah replied. She began to rock back and forth, rocking Victoria with her. They held each other and thought about Zachariah.

"Why couldn't it have been Tyler that died?" Victoria blurted out.

Savannah jerked away from her. "You don't mean that."

"Yes, I do," Victoria insisted. She pushed herself to her feet. "If someone had to die, why couldn't it have been Tyler? Why did it have to be Zach?"

Savannah stood up and snatched the letter away from Victoria. She could not bear the thought of losing Tyler. Her parents were dead. And now her brother. Tyler would not be ripped away from her too.

Suddenly Savannah remembered the blood on Tyler's letter. Was it Tyler's blood? Had he been wounded?

"Can your dark arts tell me if Tyler has been hurt?" Savannah demanded.

Victoria frowned. "You did not believe in the dark arts when I told you the Fiers were cursed."

"I still don't. Not really. But I'm frightened. What if this is Tyler's blood on the letter? What if he is dying—"

"How can you care about him after he broke off your engagement?" Victoria asked. "He hurt you so much."

"I hurt him too," Savannah said. She squeezed her sister's hand. "Please, Victoria. Help me find out if he is all right."

Victoria's eyes hardened. "All right," she said. "Come to my room at midnight. And bring the letter."

The midnight shadows danced around Savannah as she walked down the hallway holding a tallow candle. She stood outside Victoria's door as the grandfather clock downstairs chimed twelve times. Her heart beat rapidly as she tapped on the door.

Victoria opened the door halfway. "Are you sure you want me to do this?" she asked in a low voice.

"I'm sure," Savannah replied.

Victoria blew out Savannah's candle. "Come in, then."

Savannah stepped into Victoria's room and shut the door behind her. The heavy drapes were drawn. A solitary candle burned in the center of the room. Savannah noticed a bowl on the floor and a wooden box resting beside it.

Victoria crossed the room and sat on the floor in front of the candle. Savannah suddenly felt cold. She shivered.

"Sit down," Victoria ordered.

Savannah sat cross-legged on the floor across from her sister. The candle flickered between them.

"Give me the letter," Victoria said, her voice low and serious.

Savannah unfolded Tyler's letter and handed it to her sister. Victoria placed it on the floor. The candle flame cast an eerie yellow glow over the scrawled words.

"What will you do?" Savannah whispered.

"Shh!" Victoria picked up the wooden box. It creaked as she opened the lid.

She lifted a pair of chicken feet out of the box. "Kiss them," Victoria commanded.

Savannah stared at the chicken feet Victoria held in front of her. Her stomach lurched. She shook her head. "I can't."

"You must if you wish to know the truth about Tyler."

Savannah quickly touched her lips to the cold chicken feet. She shuddered.

Victoria swept the chicken feet over Tyler's letter. Then she dipped the feet into the bowl and coated them with a dark liquid. She trailed the feet over the floor, making strange markings around Tyler's letter.

"Where did you get so much ink?" Savannah asked.

"It's not ink," Victoria answered. "It's blood."

Savannah covered her mouth. "You frighten me, Victoria," she said hoarsely.

"I frighten you?" she said harshly. She picked up Tyler's letter. "This should frighten you!"

She carefully placed the letter back on the floor. She raised her hands toward the ceiling and dropped her head back. She closed her eyes, swayed from side to side, and began to repeat an incantation.

The room grew frigid. Savannah wrapped her arms around herself. I should never have asked her to do this, Savannah thought. I can feel the evil in this room.

The drapes began to flutter.

Victoria released a shrill cry.

Icy wind rushed into the room. It lifted Tyler's letter and carried it into the flickering candle flame.

"No!" Savannah cried. She reached out to grab the burning letter.

Victoria shoved Savannah away. Savannah watched helplessly as Tyler's letter crumbled into ashes.

"How could you?" Savannah demanded. "How could you let my letter burn?"

"You should be glad," Victoria said, her voice cold. "In that single moment I saw the truth."

"The truth? You know nothing about the truth or Tyler. I never should have trusted you with his letter. You still want him for yourself. You're still jealous."

Victoria grabbed Savannah by the arm. Her dark eyes glittered in the candlelight. "You must believe in the dark arts, Savannah. They reveal the truth. Tyler Fier will destroy you as easily as a single flame destroyed his letter!"

Chapter
9

"**T**yler Fier is evil!" Victoria cried. "Evil! Evil! Evil!"

"No!" Savannah yelled. She jerked away from her sister. "I don't believe that. I love Tyler and I am going to marry him."

"Bad luck follows his family," Victoria warned her. "His bad luck will follow you too."

"No!" Savannah cried, covering her ears. "I won't listen a moment longer." She fled into the darkened hallway.

Victoria doesn't know Tyler as I do, Savannah thought. She stumbled down the stairs and into the foyer. She threw open the front door. Bright moonlight poured into the house.

Savannah rushed outside. She took a deep breath of the night air. Lightning flashed in the distance and the wind picked up. It blew Savannah's hair around her face.

A storm, she realized. A storm is blowing in.

In the distance she heard a sound. A flapping sound.

Geese! she thought. We can eat geese. She ran around to the side of the house, but she didn't see any geese. Only sheets hanging on the clothesline.

Victoria forgot to bring the wash in, Savannah realized. All I heard were the sheets flapping in the wind.

The wind howled, blowing harder and harder. Savannah suddenly had the feeling that someone was watching her. She stared up at Victoria's window. It was dark and empty.

Savannah heard a loud pop. She froze. "Victoria? Did you follow me out here?"

Silence.

She thought she saw someone moving behind the sheets. She grabbed one and whipped it back.

But no one was there.

Savannah shivered. Victoria's ritual made me edgy, she thought. I never should have asked her to begin practicing her dark arts again.

Snap! A sheet blew free of the clothesline. It enveloped Savannah. It muffled her scream as it wrapped around her. Tight. So tight. It pinned her arms to her sides.

Savannah fell to the ground.

I can't breathe, she realized in a panic. I can't breathe.

She choked and gagged. The sheet filled her mouth. Blocked her nose. Suffocating her.

Chapter
10

I don't want to die! Savannah thought. Please, I don't want to die!

She fought for breath. Struggling to drag air into her aching lungs.

Savannah rolled over the ground, fighting to loosen the sheet.

The sheet snagged on something—and Savannah heard it rip. She yanked it off her.

Savannah scrambled to her feet, sucking in huge gulps of air. She looked up and saw Victoria. Her sister stood in the window, watching her.

Victoria! Why didn't she help me?

A horrible idea occurred to Savannah. Victoria did this to me, she thought. She used her dark arts to scare me—to convince me to stay away from Tyler.

The wind blew harder. The remaining sheets flapped wildly on the clothesline.

You see, Savannah scolded herself. There is a rational explanation for what happened. A storm is coming in. The wind is fierce. Victoria didn't do anything. The wind blew the sheet around me and I panicked.

Victoria loves me. She would never harm me, Savannah told herself.

Would she?

Blackrose Manor

The old woman contemplated the roses surrounding her. The black roses. As black as the ashes that remained after Tyler's letter burned.

"My story would be so much happier if Tyler's letter had never arrived," she whispered in a hoarse voice. "Everything changed after the letter came. Everything changed after it burned."

She trailed her gnarled finger over a black flannel pouch. Long ago she had pinned it to her skirt.

Its contents are supposed to ward away evil, she thought. But only if you believe. Only if you truly believe.

A pretty little bird landed on the back of her chair.

The withered woman turned slightly and looked at its bright blue feathers. They were the only thing of color in the garden.

"Do you want to hear the rest of my story?" she asked in a raspy voice.

The bird chirped.

The old woman laughed softly. "Very well, then."

The war continued. Autumn arrived. The leaves changed color. But the sisters barely noticed. They both thought often of Tyler.

Winter came. The chill winds circled the plantation. Circled the sisters. A coldness grew between Victoria and Savannah.

By spring the sisters were drifting apart.

Victoria no longer crawled into bed with Savannah when she was frightened.

Savannah often sat on the front porch steps, watching the road—waiting. Waiting for the war to end. Waiting for another letter.

"If only Tyler had not written at all." The old woman's voice caught. She stared vacantly at the roses. Black. As black as Tyler's hair. As black as—

The bluebird twittered.

The old woman grabbed the bird and tore off its tiny head.

Chapter
11

—————

Whispering Oaks
Spring 1865

The bright sun warmed Savannah as she hoed the small garden.

By summer we will have fresh corn to eat, she thought as she straightened her back. Corn, beans, and watermelon.

Yesterday she had found a few seeds in the cellar, hidden beneath dust and old crates. She wanted to plant them today.

Victoria and I will have a feast someday, Savannah thought. She asked Victoria to help with the garden, but Victoria claimed she was too busy.

"Too busy," Savannah repeated softly. "Too busy doing what?"

Savannah sighed heavily. Ever since Tyler's letter, Victoria has changed, Savannah thought. Now she scurries through the house like a frightened rat. She hides in her room. If I knock on her door, she tells me to go away.

Savannah pounded the hoe into the soil, turning the dirt over and over. A long shadow fell across the soil in front of her.

Startled, Savannah jerked her head up. She hadn't heard anyone approach.

A tall, bedraggled man stood before her. His short gray jacket and trousers were faded and hung loose on his skeletal frame. His boots were worn thin and covered in dust.

He must be a deserter, Savannah thought. She tightened her grip on the hoe and pointed away from the house. "The army is camped over there."

"No army," he said in a hoarse voice. "The war is over. I am going home."

He walked on, dragging his feet over the furrows Savannah had made with the hoe. She reached out and grabbed his arm. "What? What did you say?"

He nodded. "It's over. They told us to go home. General Lee surrendered. I am going back to Texas."

Savannah released the man, his words echoing around her.

The war is over.

"The war is truly over?" she called out to the young soldier, wanting more reassurance.

"Yes, ma'am," he replied over his shoulder as he shuffled away.

She hurried after him. "Let me get you something to drink."

"No, thank you, ma'am. I just want to go home."

Savannah closed her eyes and listened. Listened

hard. No cannons roared in the distance. No gunfire filled the air.

She could hear birds singing in the trees! Savannah waltzed across the soil, using the hoe as her dance partner. "The war is over. The war is over!"

Victoria, she thought. I must tell Victoria. She dropped the hoe and ran into the house. "Victoria! The war is over!"

Savannah rushed up the wide winding staircase and burst into Victoria's room. Then she stumbled to a halt.

What she saw caused a cold chill to slither down her back.

Victoria sat in a rocking chair near the window. Rocking. Rocking back and forth. And talking.

Talking to Tyler.

Chapter 12

"You are evil, Tyler Fier. Do you feel the sun?" Victoria asked. She laughed. "It will get hotter and hotter."

Victoria didn't hear me come into her room, Savannah realized. Her sister continued to rock and talk. Savannah inched closer.

Then she saw the wax doll on the windowsill. The wax doll that looked like Tyler.

"What are you doing, Victoria?" Savannah asked. She struggled to keep her voice calm.

"I am destroying Tyler for you," Victoria said quietly, her brown eyes dull. "Then he won't be able to hurt you."

I can't talk to her about this now, Savannah thought. She knelt in front of her sister. "Victoria, the war is over," Savannah said gently. "The soldiers will start coming home now."

53

Tears filled Victoria's eyes. "But who will come home to us? Zachariah is dead."

"Friends, neighbors . . ." Savannah answered.

"And Tyler," Victoria said, her voice cold, "I don't want him to come here. I don't want him in our house."

Victoria picked up the wax doll and carried it to her bedside table. She lit a tallow candle and held the doll's head over the flame.

Savannah watched with dismay as the doll's wax face melted.

"He's evil!" Victoria cried. She spun around and threw the doll against the wall. It fell to the floor with a thud.

I cannot convince her that Tyler is *not* evil, Savannah thought. She will just have to see the truth for herself when he returns.

If he returns. Savannah hated to think about the possibility that Tyler would not return. But she had never received another letter.

"I'm going to find us something to eat," Savannah said. "We will celebrate tonight."

She turned to leave. Victoria grabbed her arm. "Wait. I have something for you." She picked up a black flannel pouch and held it out to Savannah. "The pouch is supposed to be red, but I couldn't find any red flannel. I'm certain the black will work though."

Savannah did not take the gift. She knew from Victoria that red pouches were used to ward off evil. "What did you put inside the pouch?" she asked, dreading the answer.

"Dirt from Mother's and Father's graves. It will

protect you from evil," Victoria assured her, her eyes shining.

"I don't need protection," Savannah declared.

A few weeks later Savannah walked slowly through her garden. She searched for green sprouts, any sign that the seeds she planted would flourish.

So many soldiers had tramped through her garden, so many tired, weary soldiers trying to get home.

Maybe I should build a fence, she thought. How can my plants grow if soldiers continue to stomp across my seeds?

Tears stung Savannah's eyes. She knew they had nothing to do with the state of her garden.

I am so lonely, she thought. Victoria and I used to work together. Now I struggle alone.

A shadow fell across the soil in front of Savannah. Another soldier, she thought. Another soldier tromping across my garden. Wearily she lifted her eyes . . . and froze at the sight of the man standing before her.

Her heart thudded. I must be dreaming, she thought wildly. I am dreaming.

With trembling hands she reached out to touch the dream. But the dream was warm. The dream was firm. The dream was no dream at all.

"Tyler!" she cried. Savannah flung her arms around his neck. "Oh, Tyler! I thought you would never come back."

"Didn't you get my letter?" Tyler asked.

She leaned back until she could gaze into his blue eyes. "Yes, I got your letter."

The light left his eyes. "I'm sorry about Zachariah."

"At least you are safe," she whispered hoarsely.

"Yes," he replied, his voice low. "I am safe. And I have returned for you. I love you, Savannah." He wrapped his arms around her. "Will you marry me?"

Savannah forgot about the garden. She forgot about the empty cotton fields. She forgot about Victoria.

All she could think about was the deep blue of his eyes, begging her to say yes.

"Yes," she whispered.

He grinned. "I can't wait to show you Blackrose Manor," he told her, his voice full of excitement.

"Blackrose Manor?"

"My home in the North."

Savannah felt a weight settle in her chest.

"I love you, Savannah," he said.

I refused to follow him once, she thought. I regretted my decision for four long years. There is nothing to keep me here now. I want no more regrets in my life.

"Tyler, I want to go with you," Savannah said. "I truly do. But I cannot leave Victoria here alone."

"She will come with us. We can be happy together." He bent his head and kissed her.

It felt so good to touch him again. But doubts and worries flashed through her mind. I have to tell him about Victoria, Savannah thought. I have to tell him how she has changed.

She drew away from the kiss and touched Tyler's handsome face. His brow furrowed.

"What's wrong, Savannah?" he asked.

"It's Victoria. She's changed—"

"We have all changed," he said. He held out his

hand and showed her a long, jagged scar across his palm. "I did not have this when I left."

She covered his hand with her own, hating the thought that he had been in pain. "You're right," she said. "But I am worried that Victoria is losing her mind. She has some silly notion——"

Savannah stopped. *I can't tell him Victoria thinks he is evil. It would hurt him to know my sister doesn't trust him.*

She tried to explain. "Sometimes Victoria does strange things. But she doesn't mean any harm."

"Perhaps a change will do her good. She'll like Blackrose Manor," he assured her. "You both will."

Savannah felt joy swell within her. "I can't wait to go."

"Then we will leave tomorrow," Tyler said.

"Tomorrow," Savannah repeated. "I will tell Victoria."

Savannah found Victoria at the small family cemetery. The black pouch was pinned to Victoria's skirt.

"Tyler has returned," Victoria said in a flat voice.

Savannah grabbed her hands. "Yes. How did you know?"

Victoria did not take her eyes off the headstones. "I saw him."

Look at me, Savannah wanted to say. *Look at me so you will know that everything will be all right. Look at me so I will know you are all right.*

But Victoria's vacant gaze remained fixed on the single granite marker that bore their parents' names. Savannah released her sister's hands. "We are going to live with Tyler at Blackrose Manor," Savannah said. "We will leave the devastation of the South behind. We will have food—"

Victoria turned suddenly. "Be quiet!" she whispered harshly. "Be quiet. Listen closely. Do you not hear the wind whispering through the oak trees? Whispering the secrets, the truth?"

Victoria's voice dipped lower. "If we go to Blackrose Manor, one of us will be buried there before the year is out!"

PART TWO

Blackrose Manor
Massachussetts,
Spring 1865

Chapter
13

Lightning flashed. Thunder rumbled. Harsh wind rocked the buggy.

Savannah tightened her hold on Tyler's arm. "Will we arrive before the storm?" she asked.

"It's not much farther," Tyler told her. "I think we'll make it."

Savannah glanced over her shoulder at Victoria. She sat huddled in the backseat. She clutched the black pouch pinned to her skirt so tightly that her knuckles turned white.

Poor Victoria, Savannah thought. She is terrified. She truly believes Tyler is evil—and that one of us will die at Blackrose Manor.

Savannah wished she could reassure Victoria. But she knew nothing she could say would make her sister feel better.

Tyler stopped the buggy. He climbed out and opened a tall wrought iron gate.

We're here, Savannah thought. She leaned forward, but all she could see was the massive fence. Thorny roses climbed up the bars.

"Look, Victoria. Have you ever seen such dark red roses? They look almost black."

"I don't like this place, Savannah," Victoria said.

Savannah reached back and squeezed Victoria's hand. "The storm is probably making you nervous," she said. But she knew the storm wasn't what was bothering her sister.

The buggy swayed as Tyler climbed back in. He flicked the reins and guided the horse through the open gate.

A gust of wind swept some rose petals into the buggy. One settled on Savannah's lap. She picked up the soft petal and studied it.

I was wrong, she thought. The roses aren't dark red. They aren't red at all. "I have never seen black roses," Savannah said.

"They grow everywhere here," Tyler said. "The manor took its name from the roses." He pointed forward. "There is your new home."

Savannah gasped. The huge manor was made of cold gray stone. Its two turrets pierced the darkening sky.

Savannah wanted to like Blackrose Manor. But she thought the mansions in the South—with their wide porches and graceful columns—were much more welcoming.

Tyler brought the horse to a halt. He stepped out of

the buggy. A moment later he opened Savannah's door and offered her his arm.

They walked up the massive stone steps that led to the front door. Victoria followed.

Tyler pulled open the thick wood door. Savannah cautiously made her way down the hall to the main room while Tyler held the door for her sister.

Candles flickered in chandeliers hanging high above her. But they weren't enough to light the large room.

Savannah stared around her, trying to take in everything at once. She noticed a row of portraits along one wall. She headed toward it—then she stopped with a small cry of surprise. She pressed her hand to her throat.

A thin woman stood in a far doorway. Her iron-gray dress matched the iron-gray hair she had pulled back into a tight knot.

She was so thin that her skin appeared to be stretched tight over the bones of her face. It is like looking at a skull, Savannah thought.

"Good evening, Mrs. Mooreland." Tyler came up behind Savannah and rested his hand on her shoulder. "I want you to meet Savannah. As you know, we are to be married."

Tyler turned toward Victoria and reached for her hand. She backed away. He shrugged. "And this sweet lady is Victoria—Savannah's sister."

"Why would anyone choose to live here?" Victoria whispered. "It is so cold and gloomy."

Savannah gave Victoria a warning look. "We're guests here," she said softly.

"Not for long," Tyler corrected her. He smiled and slipped his arm around her. "Once we are married, you will be my wife, not my guest. And Victoria will be my sister."

He is trying so hard to make Victoria feel at home. I wish she would give him a chance, Savannah thought.

"I have to see after the horse and buggy. Mrs. Mooreland, please show Savannah and Victoria to their rooms." Tyler brushed his lips over Savannah's cheek. "I leave you in capable hands," he murmured.

Mrs. Mooreland didn't say a word. She stared at Savannah. Her face grim, her eyes cold.

Savannah grabbed Victoria's hand—and her sister didn't pull away. "Would you show us to our rooms, please?" she asked.

Mrs. Mooreland narrowed her black eyes. "Very well. Follow me."

With efficient clicks of her heels, Mrs. Mooreland led them to a winding stone staircase.

"This place frightens me," Victoria said as they followed Mrs. Mooreland up the stairs.

Savannah squeezed her sister's hand. "We will be all right," she promised.

Mrs. Mooreland glanced over her bony shoulder. "Take care on the stairs. Over the years the stone has grown smooth and slippery."

"Thank you for the warning, Mrs. Mooreland," Savannah replied.

The servant merely nodded and continued up the steps.

"Please, Savannah, let's return to Whispering Oaks. Before it is too late," Victoria begged.

"Whispering Oaks is no more," Savannah answered harshly. "You know that. Our home is here."

"But I can feel the evil in this house . . . lurking in the shadows," Victoria said in a hushed voice.

"Nonsense," Savannah said. "We will simply add more candles to the chandeliers and chase the shadows away."

"I don't think candles will make a difference," Victoria said.

"Everything will be all right once we get used to it," Savannah promised. She hoped she was telling the truth.

At the top of the stairs Mrs. Mooreland threw open a door. "One of the guest rooms."

"I'll take this room," Victoria said. She scurried into the room and closed the door.

"She is wise to hide," Mrs. Mooreland said.

Savannah was taken aback by the woman's words. The servants at Whispering Oaks would never have made a comment like that. "And where is my room?" Savannah asked firmly, ignoring the woman's remark.

Mrs. Mooreland crossed the hall and opened another door. "In here."

Savannah stepped inside. A fire burned in the hearth—but the room still felt cold and damp. Black draperies hid the windows. A black quilt covered the beds.

I feel as though I am at a funeral, Savannah thought. Why are there no colors in this house? Why is everything so cold?

She turned to ask Mrs. Mooreland, but stopped. She did not want the servant to know that she felt uncomfortable in Tyler's home.

She placed her hands on her hips and smiled. "Well,

I can see that my first order of business will be to bring some color to these rooms."

Mrs. Mooreland didn't reply. The sound of her raspy breathing filled the room. She moved closer to Savannah and leaned down—so she could stare directly into Savannah's eyes.

Savannah's first instinct was to back away. But she forced herself to remain where she was and return Mrs. Mooreland's stare.

"You are not wanted here," the housekeeper said. "Leave while you can."

Chapter
14
_____

Savannah felt her stomach twist inside her. What a cruel thing to say, she thought. But she kept her face blank. She would not allow Mrs. Mooreland to see that her words had hurt Savannah.

She tilted up her chin defiantly. "Thank you, Mrs. Mooreland. You may return to your other duties."

Without another word, the servant walked out of the room and closed the door behind her.

Savannah hurried to the hearth. A low fire crackled in the wide stone fireplace. She knelt before the fire and held her hands before the orange flames.

This house is so cold, Savannah thought. Her bones felt as if they had frozen inside her.

I expected Tyler's home to be like Whispering Oaks before the war, she thought sadly. A happy place, filled with warmth and color and gaiety.

She shuddered. And I expected a warm welcome.

Why was Mrs. Mooreland so unkind? Why didn't Lucy come downstairs to meet us?

Tyler had told Savannah that Lucy was like a little sister to him. His parents became her guardians when Lucy's parents were killed. Now Tyler felt responsible for the girl.

Savannah shivered. I must find Tyler, she thought as she stood. I must talk with him. Something isn't right here.

She walked out of her room. Candles flickered in chandeliers overhead. She heard something scrape across stone. Then she heard a crash from the first floor.

She rushed to the staircase and took the slippery stairs as quickly as she dared. Halfway down she saw something so frightening that she had to press her hands against her mouth to keep from screaming.

What is he doing? What is Tyler doing?

Tyler paced back and forth across the main room. He held a large butcher knife high in his hand. His face was twisted in fury.

"Stop staring at me!" he snarled. "Stop staring at me or I will cut your eyes out!"

Chapter
15

Tyler lifted one of the portraits off the wall and threw it down. He attacked it with the butcher knife, stabbing it over and over.

Savannah stood frozen halfway down the stairs. She gathered her courage. "Tyler?" she called gently.

He stopped, his hand in midair, the knife poised above the portrait. Savannah felt her heart quicken as he turned, his eyes filled with pain.

"They don't understand, Savannah," he moaned. "They don't understand that I did what I had to do during the war."

Savannah hurried down the rest of the stairs. She gazed at the portraits that still lined the wall. Portraits of Tyler's ancestors.

"It doesn't matter if they understand," she said. She took a few steps toward Tyler. "I understand."

"You can't understand," Tyler insisted. "There was

so much killing . . . so much blood. You would hate me if you knew the things I've done."

"I could never hate you," Savannah said. "During the war we all did what we had to do to survive." She inched closer. "But now the war is over."

The knife clattered to the floor. Tyler jerked her to him and wrapped his arms around her. "I never want to see blood again," he said in a shaky voice.

Savannah stroked his black hair away from his forehead. "Victoria and I had to eat worms," she told him, hoping to make him smile.

He laughed. Savannah could feel his chest shaking under his shirt.

She tilted her face and gazed into his blue eyes. "Together we can put the war behind us," she whispered.

"Yes," he replied. "Together we can."

He lowered his mouth to hers. Savannah returned his kiss eagerly. I love him so much, she thought. He is all I have ever wanted.

Savannah heard a high-pitched shriek. She jerked away from Tyler.

The shrill cry came again.

It took Savannah a moment to realize the sound was Victoria screaming.

Chapter
16

Savannah heard footsteps pounding down the staircase.

A young girl in a black dress appeared. "Tyler, save me!" she cried as she raced downstairs and flung herself into Tyler's arms.

Victoria screamed again. She flew down the last few steps. "Give me my pouch," Victoria cried. She lunged for the girl.

Savannah grabbed her sister's shoulders and held her back. She could feel Victoria trembling. "I need my pouch, Savannah. I'm not safe here without it. I need protection from the evil. Please, please make her give it back to me."

"Is that true, Lucy?" Tyler asked. "Did you take something that belongs to Victoria?"

So this is Lucy, Savannah realized. She is just a child.

"Answer me, Lucy," Tyler said firmly.

Lucy nodded. "But I only wanted to look inside," she said. "I wasn't going to keep it."

"Give it back, and say you are sorry," Tyler instructed. "There is nothing Lucy likes better than finding out secrets," he added to Savannah. "She creeps around here as quiet as a little mouse, hoping to hear something interesting."

Lucy held out the pouch, and Victoria snatched it away. "I'm sorry," Lucy said in high little voice.

Victoria didn't answer. She frantically tried to repin the pouch onto her skirt. "Let me," Savannah said. She pinned the pouch firmly in place.

Savannah didn't like to encourage Victoria in her strange beliefs. But if Victoria believed the pouch could protect her from evil, Savannah thought it was harmless. She wanted her sister to be happy at Blackrose Manor.

"Lucy, this is Miss Savannah Gentry and Miss Victoria Gentry. Remember I wrote and told you they will be living with us from now on."

Lucy peered up at Savannah. Her curly black hair framed her young face. "Did your mother and father die too?" Lucy asked. "That's why *I* came to live here."

"Yes, they did." Savannah's heart went out to the young girl whose black eyes held such sadness. Lucy can't be more than thirteen, Savannah thought to herself. So very young to be an orphan.

Tyler eased the girl away from his side. "Go on back upstairs and get ready for supper. I want to talk to Miss Savannah alone."

Lucy reluctantly crossed the room and started up

the stairs. Savannah gave Victoria a little nudge, and her sister followed the younger girl.

Tyler picked up the ruined portrait and the butcher knife from the floor. "I was hoping Victoria and Lucy wouldn't notice these."

"They were too involved in their argument to pay any attention," Savannah reassured him.

"Do you like your room?" he asked. She could tell that he wanted to please her.

"I like the room," she said softly. "But, Tyler, why is everything black?"

He sighed deeply. "It was my father's doing. When my mother died, he said the house went into mourning. He ordered the whole house decorated in black. We can change it now that you're here."

Savannah decided not to tell Tyler about Mrs. Mooreland's rude behavior. There had been enough upheaval for one day.

"I guess I should go up and get ready for supper too," Savannah said. Tyler nodded. She could feel him watching her as she climbed back up the stairs.

Savannah stood in front of the mirror, admiring her blue satin gown. A gift from Tyler.

She turned slightly and looked over her shoulder at her reflection. She had brushed her blond hair until it was as shiny as silk.

This is the way life was before the war, Savannah thought. Wearing beautiful clothes. Getting ready for a special dinner. Feeling pretty.

She strolled out of her room and down the hall to Victoria's door. She knocked, and Victoria answered, wearing a deep purple dress.

I'm glad Tyler thought to give Victoria a dress too. How could I go down to dinner dressed this way if Victoria was still in one our shabby old dresses.

"You look beautiful," Savannah exclaimed. "Are you ready to go downstairs?"

Victoria nodded. She ran her fingers over her flannel pouch.

Savannah led the way downstairs. She wrapped her arms around herself as she tried to decide where the dining room would be.

"You feel it too, don't you?" Victoria asked in a low voice. "There's something strange about this place. It's so cold and dark. All these fires and there is no warmth. All the candles in this room and there is so little light."

Savannah rubbed her hands up and down her arms. "It's an old house. It's drafty, that's all."

"This way, Savannah," she heard Tyler call. She followed his voice down the hall and into a formal dining room

Savannah felt like groaning when she saw the black cloth covering the long table. I must do something about all this black, she thought.

Tyler stepped toward her, an appreciative smile on his face. "You look beautiful tonight, Savannah."

Savannah felt herself blush as Tyler took her hand and brought it to his lips. "So beautiful," he whispered. He led her to a place near the head of the table. "I want you to sit next to me. And, Victoria, you sit on my other side," he added quickly.

Lucy ran in and gave a little squeak as Victoria sat down. "That's my place!" she exclaimed.

"Tonight it is Victoria's," Tyler said. "You may sit there tomorrow night."

Lucy pouted. "May I at least light the candles, then?" she asked.

"No, I will light them," Mrs. Mooreland said as she entered the room. With an enormous sigh Lucy plopped down in the chair next to Victoria.

Mrs. Mooreland lit the candelabrum. A maid appeared with a tureen of soup and served them each a portion.

Savannah's mouth watered. Her stomach tightened. It has been so long since I have had a real dinner, she thought.

"Everything smells delicious, Mrs. Mooreland," Tyler said.

"Thank you, sir," Mrs. Mooreland said before she hurried from the room.

Savannah glanced at Victoria. Her pouch rested beside her plate. She turned it over and over, constantly touching it.

"Tyler is going to teach me how to ride," Lucy announced excitedly.

Savannah turned her attention to Lucy. "That's wonderful. Victoria and I have been riding since we were young. Haven't we, Victoria?" she asked, trying to draw Victoria's attention away from her pouch.

"Yes," Victoria said without glancing up.

"Tyler is going to teach me to play the piano too," Lucy said.

Lucy has a crush on Tyler, Savannah realized. How adorable she is. Every sentence she utters has Tyler's name in it.

Savannah took a few sips of her soup. Savoring every vegetable, every spice. Before she could finish, Mrs. Mooreland appeared with the main course—veal and oysters.

As the housekeeper served, Savannah noticed Lucy staring at the candle flames. She could see the flames reflected in Lucy's dark eyes.

Slowly, Lucy reached toward the flames. Her fingers inching closer and closer.

Victoria slapped Lucy's hand away. "Stop that!" she ordered.

Lucy wrinkled her tiny nose. "I don't have to listen to you."

"Lucy, behave yourself," Tyler admonished, his voice stern.

Lucy slumped forward. "She's not my mother."

"Victoria just didn't want you to hurt yourself," Savannah said, pleased that Tyler had sided with her sister.

We will become a family, the four of us, Savannah thought. Together—

A quiet giggle interrupted her thoughts.

She glanced over at Lucy. She was staring at the candle flames again. Staring hard.

Lucy shot out her hand and knocked the candelabrum over.

"Fire!" Lucy cried. "Fire!"

Chapter
17

Savannah leapt from her chair. It fell over with a crash.

She slapped out the flames with her linen napkin. The smell of scorched cloth filled the dining room.

Savannah sighed at the sight of the singed tablecloth. It was damaged beyond repair.

"It was an accident," Lucy whispered hoarsely.

"No, it wasn't. You did it on purpose. I saw you," Victoria scolded.

Lucy raised her eyes to Savannah. "But the flames are so pretty. I like the way they dance."

Savannah's heart went out to the child. *How can I blame her for finding beauty in the flames when they are the only thing of color in this house?*

She picked up her chair and sat back down. "They are pretty, but they are also dangerous. You must not play with the candles anymore."

"Savannah is right. Go up to bed, Lucy," Tyler said in a stern voice.

Lucy slipped out of her chair and hurried over to Tyler. "Are you angry with me?" she asked.

She adores him, Savannah thought again.

"Yes," Tyler answered. Then he tweaked her nose. "But I won't stay angry long."

Lucy's face broke out into a wide grin. "I love you, Tyler," she cried. Then she skipped out of the room.

"She's sweet," Savannah said as they continued with the main course.

"She is a spoiled brat," Victoria said. She tossed her napkin onto the table. "I am going to bed." She walked from the room.

Savannah turned to Tyler. "It's been quite an exciting first day."

Tyler touched her cheek. "You look tired."

"I am," she admitted. "As soon as we finish our meal, I think I'll go on to bed too."

Savannah thought she would fall asleep immediately. But she lay awake a long time.

My first night in my new home, she thought. Blackrose Manor wasn't at all what she had expected.

Glowing red embers flew onto the stone hearth with a pop. They burned brightly. Then turned black and died.

Everything is so dark here. So gloomy. It's little wonder Victoria is uncomfortable here. Maybe I should redecorate her room first.

Savannah stretched her toes toward the warming pan at the foot of her bed. Mrs. Mooreland had brought the pan at Tyler's request. It had been obvious from her puckered lips that she would have preferred not to go to the trouble. What can I do about Mrs. Mooreland? she wondered.

Savannah yawned. So many things to think about. Victoria. Mrs. Mooreland. Lucy and her fascination with fire.

And Tyler. She was frightened when he attacked the portrait. He looked so fierce and angry.

But I can't expect him to be exactly the same after the war, Savannah thought. After years of blood and killing.

And he has been so wonderful in so many other ways. Savannah could tell he truly wanted her and Victoria to be happy.

She heard the gentle strains of a violin floating toward her. She sighed softly. I wonder if that is Tyler playing?

It was her last thought as she drifted off to sleep.

Something cold brushed against Savannah's cheek. She still felt tired, too tired to open her eyes.

A draft, she thought. This room is filled with drafts.

The cold touch came again. Cold and *wet*. What is that?

Savannah opened her eyes. She saw a calico tail swishing back and forth at the top of her quilt.

Savannah sat up and pulled back the covers. A small cat stared up at her. It nudged her cheek with its cold little nose.

"Where did you come from?" she asked.

The cat purred and licked her hand with its rough tongue. Savannah smiled.

The door opened and a young woman wearing a black uniform ran in. She wore her bright red hair in two braids beneath a white lace cap. Light freckles dotted her face.

Her gray eyes widened and she came to a dead stop when she saw that Savannah was awake. She bobbed a quick curtsy.

"Oh, miss, I am so sorry. The cat slipped away from me."

Savannah stroked the cat's fur. Its purr vibrated low in its throat. "Don't be silly. He's sweet. What's his name?"

"Calico." The young woman blushed.

"I like the name," Savannah told her.

The woman bobbed another curtsy. "My name is Hattie."

"I'm Savannah."

"Yes, miss, I know. Mr. Fier hired me this morning as a maid for you and your sister." Her cheeks pinkened as she peered at Savannah through her long lashes. "He told me you were the pretty one."

Savannah felt herself blush at Tyler's compliment. He is certainly spoiling me, she thought. I should do something special for him. But what?

She remembered his smile as she walked into the dining room wearing the blue gown. I will wear it again this evening, she thought.

"Hattie, would you do me a favor? Would you press my blue silk dress for me? It's hanging in the closet."

Hattie bobbed up and down. "Certainly, miss." With a light bounce in her step, she crossed the room and opened the closet door.

"The dress is lovely, isn't it?" Savannah asked when she heard Hattie's quick intake of breath.

Hattie turned to face her. All color had drained from the girl's face.

"What is it, Hattie?" Savannah cried. "What's wrong?"

Chapter
18

"The dress, miss. It's . . . it's . . ." Hattie reached into the closet and pulled the dress out. She held it up for Savannah to see.

Savannah gasped in disbelief. Long, jagged tears ran from the shoulders to the hem.

Savannah eased the cat off her lap and slipped out of bed. She shuddered as her feet hit the ice-cold stone floor.

"Oh, no," she murmured as she ran her fingers over the rips. Her beautiful dress! How did this happen? Savannah wondered. It couldn't have been an accident.

"Your dress is ruined!"

Startled by Lucy's voice, Savannah spun around. The younger girl had come in without knocking and was staring at the dress.

How long had she been there? Savannah wondered. Was she listening outside the door?

"Tyler gave you that dress, didn't he?" Lucy asked.

"Yes, he did," Savannah said.

Lucy frowned. "He said you were beautiful. He'll be sad when he finds out it was ruined."

"Yes, he will be sad," Savannah replied. "So I don't want to tell him. I want to keep it a secret."

Lucy's eyes glittered. "I'm good at keeping secrets." She reached out and took Savannah's hand. "I'm so glad you're finally awake. I want to show you my doll collection."

"I will get dressed," Savannah told her.

"But I've been waiting all morning. Please come now."

Lucy's excitement was contagious. I'm glad that she lived so far north, away from the war. It would have changed her so.

"All right," Savannah said. She pulled on her dressing gown. "Show me your dolls."

Lucy tugged Savannah across the hall. "This is my room," she said with pride. She opened the door and skipped in.

Savannah followed Lucy into the room, not surprised to find the room decorated in black.

It was wrong to do this to a child's room, she thought. And Lucy is still a child. Her room was filled with dolls—on the bed, on the dresser, on the shelves, on the floor. Porcelain dolls. Rag dolls.

A cold draft caused goose bumps to form along Savannah's arms. All the dolls had black hair like Lucy's, she noticed. All the dolls had black eyes. All the dolls wore black dresses.

Are the dolls all in mourning just like this house? she wondered. What a joyless place for a child to grow up.

Lucy flung herself across her bed. Two dolls leaning against the headboard fell forward. Lucy picked one up and hugged it close against her.

"These are all my friends," Lucy said solemnly. "Tyler always brings me a new doll every time he goes away."

Savannah sat on the edge of the bed. How sad that Lucy doesn't have any real friends. "I would like to be your friend too," she said.

Lucy's forehead wrinkled. "I don't think you can."

"Why not?" Savannah asked. She tried not to feel hurt. Lucy would need some time to get used to her.

Lucy shook her head. "We can't be friends because Tyler brought you here to live. So we're almost sisters. I have always wanted a sister. I think a sister would be much better than a friend."

Savannah hugged Lucy close. "I have always wanted another sister."

Lucy hopped off the bed and picked up a rag doll from a rocking chair. The doll was as tall as Lucy.

"Tyler gave me this doll first," she said, smiling brightly. "Don't you think she's pretty?"

"She's very pretty," Savannah assured her. "What's her name?"

"Her name is Lucy." She dropped the doll back into the chair. "Which doll do you like best?"

Savannah pretended to consider the question with great seriousness. "I'm not sure," she said. She stood and tapped her finger against her lips. "They are all so pretty."

"You have to pick one," Lucy insisted.

Savannah walked around the room, studying all the dolls. Lucy grinned with delight.

Savannah spotted a doll lying on its side on top of the dresser bureau. Its profile was perfect: a small nose, a ruddy cheek, thin lips, a large, shining black eye.

I'll pick this doll, Savannah decided. She lifted it up and gasped.

The other side of the doll's face was smashed in. Tiny bits of jagged china formed a gaping hole where the eye had been.

"What happened to this doll?" Savannah asked Lucy.

"I killed her."

Chapter
19

Lucy's black eyes were big and serious. Savannah felt a chill sweep through her.

Then Lucy began to giggle. "I didn't really kill her. She fell off the bureau. That's how she broke her face."

Savannah released her breath with a *whoosh*.

Lucy sighed. "She was the prettiest doll. The other dolls were happy when she got hurt."

She's teasing me, Savannah thought, fighting off a feeling of alarm. "They weren't really happy," Savannah said.

"Yes, they were," Lucy insisted. "They were very happy Lucy got hurt."

Savannah felt confused. "I thought the big doll in the rocker was named Lucy."

"Silly Savannah," Lucy exclaimed. "All the dolls are named Lucy."

Lucy glanced around the room. Then she leaned close to Savannah. "Except one," she whispered. Lucy crooked her finger. "Follow me."

Savannah set the porcelain doll back on the dresser and followed Lucy to the closet. Lucy opened the door and pulled out a large doll.

"This is Tyler," she said proudly. She sat down and placed the doll in her lap.

Savannah studied the strange doll. Its black hair was cropped short and was longer on one side than the other. Its clothes were a little too big. And its eyes. Its eyes were blue.

"He does look like Tyler," Savannah told Lucy.

"I made him," Lucy explained. "I told Tyler I wanted a boy doll, but he always brought me girl dolls. So I cut off this doll's hair. And one day when Mrs. Mooreland made blueberry cobbler, I stole some juice and painted the eyes blue."

"That was very clever," Savannah said, impressed by Lucy's efforts.

"And I snuck into the attic and found some of the clothes Tyler wore when he was tiny," she said. Her eyes gleamed. "Don't tell Tyler. He doesn't like me sneaking though the house."

Savannah smiled. "Since you're keeping my secret about the dress, it's only fair that I keep your secret about the doll."

"I like sharing secrets," Lucy whispered. "Someday I will tell you all the secrets."

Secrets, Savannah thought as she left Lucy's room and crossed the hall. When I was Lucy's age, I loved secrets too. But I shared all my secrets with Victoria.

She opened the door to her room and froze. Victoria stood beside her bed, slipping something beneath her pillow.

"Victoria, what are you doing?" Savannah demanded.

Victoria jumped away from the bed. "Nothing."

Savannah crossed the room in quick strides. She grabbed her pillow and lifted it.

Tiny dots of blood stained the pillow. And in the center rested something wet and spongy. A tiny eyeball!

"Oh, Victoria, what have you done?" Savannah asked. She couldn't tear her gaze from the dark brown eye.

"It's a hawk's eye," Victoria explained. "It will protect you from the evil."

"I don't need protection!" Savannah snapped. She snatched up the eye, shuddering as its coldness seeped into her palm.

"No!" Victoria cried.

Savannah threw the eye into the fire. It hissed and sizzled. Good, Savannah thought.

Savannah wiped her hand on the pillowcase. Then she pulled off the case and tossed it on the floor.

"Victoria, you must stop this," Savannah demanded. Then she looked closely at her sister for the first time since she entered the room.

Savannah's anger drained away. "Your hair," she gasped. "Victoria, what happened to your hair?"

A thick white streak ran through Victoria's brown hair.

Victoria sank onto the bed, pressing her hands against her face. "It's the evil," she murmured. "The evil in this house is powerful. It did this to me."

My poor sister, Savannah thought. She knelt in front of Victoria. "Some women get white hair at our age. Remember Mrs. Speergen?"

"No! It's the evil. I felt its cold touch during the night."

"The fire in your hearth must have gone out," Savannah insisted. Everything has an explanation, Savannah thought. Everything.

"All this black doesn't help either," Savannah said. "That will be our first job—redecorating the whole house. We'll start with your room. When we're done, Blackrose Manor will be as cozy and warm as Whispering Oaks."

"No!" Victoria stood and began pacing. "You don't understand. If we stay here, one of us will die! *Die*, Savannah."

She is so frightened. She wants to leave so desperately, Savannah realized. What would she do to convince me to leave the manor? Would she destroy the dress Tyler gave me?

Savannah rose and walked to her closet. She pulled out the ruined dress. "Victoria, did you do this?" she asked gently. "Did you hope to frighten me into leaving? I will understand if you did. I promise."

"No!" she exclaimed. Then her eyes narrowed. "I bet Lucy tore up your dress. She's jealous of you because she wants Tyler for herself."

"Lucy is just a child," she protested. "She has a young girl's crush on Tyler. Nothing more."

"A child!" Victoria exclaimed. "Lucy is no little girl. She is seventeen. The same age you were when you met Tyler. And Lucy will do anything to have him all to herself!"

Chapter
20

Seventeen!

Could Victoria be right? she wondered.

"But her clothes are those of a child," Savannah protested. "And her dolls. Have you seen her doll collection?"

Victoria rolled her eyes. "And she is fascinated with fire. Have you forgotten how she played with the candles last night? She is strange, Savannah, but she is seventeen. And she is in love with Tyler."

Savannah ran her hand along the torn dress. Is Lucy in love with Tyler? Is she so jealous of the compliments Tyler paid me last night that she destroyed my dress?

Victoria grabbed Savannah by both arms, her fingernails digging into Savannah's skin.

"Ow!" Savannah yelped.

"Let Lucy have Tyler," Victoria cried. "Let all the bad luck stay in their family!"

"I love Tyler, and nothing will stop me from marrying him," Savannah declared. She yanked away from Victoria. "Nothing!"

Tyler's voice boomed up the stairs. "Everyone! Come outside! I have a surprise for Savannah!"

"I'm not even dressed," Savannah exclaimed. "Victoria, please go downstairs and tell Tyler I'll be there in a few moments."

Savannah could see Victoria hesitate. "Please," she begged.

Victoria heaved a sigh. "All right."

Savannah watched her sister shuffle out of the room. Then she hurried to dress.

Another surprise, she thought as she rushed downstairs. I don't know how many more surprises I can bear.

Savannah found Victoria, Lucy, Hattie, and Mrs. Mooreland on the front steps. Then she saw Tyler. She couldn't believe her eyes.

Tyler was leading the most beautiful horse she had ever seen straight toward her. He stopped in front of Savannah and patted the black stallion's neck. "He's yours," Tyler said with a grin.

Savannah glanced around at the others. Only Hattie had a smile on her face.

What is wrong with everyone else? Can't Tyler give me a present without them all getting jealous?

Savannah climbed down the steps and cautiously approached the horse. He snorted. Startled, Savannah jumped back.

Tyler pulled Savannah close to him. "Don't be

afraid," he said. "He is as gentle as a lamb. I've named him Whisper in honor of your father's plantation."

Savannah spun around. "Victoria, did you hear that?"

"I heard," Victoria said coldly. "It means nothing." She walked into the house.

I won't let her spoil my wonderful gift, Savannah decided. "Can we go for a ride?" she asked Tyler. "Just one quick ride before breakfast. Please."

"One quick ride." He gave her a kiss, then lifted her onto the horse.

As Tyler mounted his own horse, Lucy walked over to Savannah. She tilted her head back and placed her hand gently on Savannah's leg. "I think Tyler likes you best of all," Lucy whispered.

Savannah glanced at Tyler. He winked at her.

"Keep breakfast warm, Mrs. Mooreland," he instructed the housekeeper. "We won't be long. Now, Savannah, let's see if you can keep up with me."

He kicked his horse into a canter. Savannah shrieked at his unfair head start.

"I will not only keep up with you, Tyler Fier," she yelled as she urged her horse into a gallop. "I will outrun you!"

An hour later, breathless and laughing, Savannah walked into the dining room with Tyler.

"Who won the race?" Lucy asked as she took her place at the table.

"I think it was a tie," Tyler said. He patted Lucy's head.

"I think I won," Savannah teased.

"Savannah!" Lucy cried. "Sit by me!"

Lucy's excited request took Savannah by surprise. It's so strange to think of Lucy as seventeen. She looks like a little girl waiting to open a birthday present.

"Please," Lucy prodded.

Before Savannah could respond, Tyler answered for her. "Savannah can sit with you this morning. But in the future, I want her to sit by me."

Reluctantly Savannah eased herself into the chair beside Lucy. Victoria sat down across from her.

Does Lucy want my company? Savannah wondered. Or does she want to keep me away from Tyler?

"Savannah should always sit beside me," Lucy piped in. "We're sisters. Savannah told me she always wanted a different sister."

Victoria gasped.

"Was that supposed to be a secret?" Lucy asked, her dark eyes wide and innocent.

Savannah saw the hurt in Victoria's eyes. "Lucy misunderstood what I said," Savannah explained. "I simply meant it would be nice to have two sisters."

Victoria nodded. She began pushing her food around her plate without eating anything.

Victoria doesn't understand, Savannah thought. Her feelings are still hurt.

Savannah took a few bites of scrambled eggs, but the food stuck in her mouth. She hated it when Victoria was upset with her.

Mrs. Mooreland hurried in and poured coffee into Tyler's cup. "The eggs are wonderful, Mrs. Mooreland," Savannah said, hoping to win her over.

Mrs. Mooreland's lips thinned. "I want your stay to be pleasant." She walked out of the room.

My stay? Savannah asked herself. She made it sound as though I would be leaving shortly. Has she forgotten that I will stay here forever?

Savannah cut off a piece of sausage. The spicy aroma hit her nose. "The sausage smells good. You should try it, Victoria," she said, hoping to lighten Victoria's mood.

Victoria rolled the sausage around on her plate but didn't take a bite.

Savannah was about to pop her own sausage into her mouth, when she felt something soft brush against her ankle. She glanced beneath the table and saw Hattie's calico cat looking up at her expectantly.

Savannah smiled. She slipped the piece of sausage off her fork and offered it to the cat. The cat devoured it greedily, then licked Savannah's hand.

"Would you like some more?" she asked.

The cat purred and rubbed against Savannah's leg. Savannah sliced off another piece of sausage.

"Savannah, will you play with me this afternoon?" Lucy asked.

What should I do? Savannah thought. Is Lucy trying to keep me away from Tyler? "Perhaps Victoria and I could play with you," Savannah suggested, hoping to make Victoria more comfortable at Blackrose Manor.

"I can't," Victoria said quickly. She rubbed her black pouch between her palms. "I need to find a better way to protect us from the evil."

Savannah was embarrassed. She wished Victoria wouldn't speak of the evil in front of Tyler. "Victoria, I've told you that there is—"

Savannah heard a choking sound from under the table. She knelt on the floor and lifted the tablecloth.

Calico bared his teeth and hissed at her. His back was arched, the fur standing on end.

"What's wrong, kitty cat?" Savannah crooned.

Calico gagged. His body convulsed, the spasms throwing him onto his side.

Then the little cat's body went still.

"Calico!" Savannah cried. "Calico is dead!"

Chapter
21

Savannah carefully lifted Calico onto her lap.

She heard footsteps, then Hattie ran into the room and dropped to her knees beside Savannah. Tears pooled in Hattie's eyes. She ran her fingers through Calico's thick fur.

"Oh, miss!" she cried. "He's not dead. I can feel him breathing."

Savannah sighed with relief. "Thank goodness. Let's take him to the kitchen. It will be warmer in there." She cradled Calico next to her chest and hurried into the kitchen. Hattie stayed beside her, crooning to her cat.

Savannah glanced around the kitchen. A large cast iron cookstove dominated one side of the room. A wood box sat beside it.

"Hattie, take the wood out of the wood box and

we'll use that as a bed for Calico," Savannah suggested.

"Yes, miss," Hattie said. She hurried to the wood box and began piling the wood onto the floor.

"You can call me Savannah," Savannah told Hattie as she knelt beside the box.

"Oh, no, miss. That wouldn't be proper." Hattie went to the pantry and came back with some old blankets. She stuffed them into the box.

Savannah placed Calico on the blankets. Hattie covered him up with one corner. "I wonder how he got sick," Hattie said.

Savannah shook her head. "I don't know. I fed him a bit of sausage—" She stopped. Could the sausage have been spoiled? she wondered.

She placed her hand on Hattie's shoulder. "Why don't you stay with Calico for a while?"

Hattie smiled. "Thank you, miss."

Savannah stood and walked back into the dining room. She stopped short at the sight of Tyler angrily questioning Mrs. Mooreland.

Victoria hurried over to Savannah and clutched her arm. "Now you see why we cannot stay here," Victoria whispered. "Someone tried to poison you!"

A few nights later Savannah stood before her window and stared down into the rose garden. The moonlight glinted on the black roses.

Savannah's stomach rumbled. She had eaten very little since Calico became ill. Mrs. Mooreland insisted that the sausage had simply gone bad. Tyler believed her.

Savannah wasn't so sure. Calico was still weak, still

lying in a box in the kitchen. Could bad sausage have made him that sick?

Is Victoria right? she wondered. Did someone try to poison me?

She pulled the drapes closed and climbed into bed. She closed her eyes. Faces circled through her mind.

Lucy's pale, innocent face. Mrs. Mooreland's stern face. Victoria's frightened face.

Did one of them try to kill me? she wondered.

Chapter
22

Savannah kicked off her blankets.

So warm. Too warm.

This house is never hot, she thought foggily. Still half asleep. Never.

She forced her eyes open—and screamed.

Bright orange flames devoured the curtains on her window.

Smoke surrounded Savannah. It filled her nose and mouth. She tried to scream again, but she could only gasp. Gasp for help. Gasp for air.

The thick gray smoke burned her eyes.

Savannah scrambled out of bed and fell to her knees, coughing and gagging. Tears streamed down her face.

The fire roared as the flames climbed up the thick drapes.

Frantically Savannah pulled herself up. She

grabbed her comforter. She could use it to beat out the fire.

One end caught on the bed frame. Savannah gave the comforter a hard tug. It ripped free—and she stumbled backward. Into the flaming curtains.

The sleeve of her nightgown caught fire.

Savannah released another hoarse scream. The door to her room burst open. Victoria rushed in. She shoved Savannah onto the bed and smothered the fire on her sleeve.

"Grab a pillow!" Savannah cried. "We have to stop the fire from spreading."

Together the sisters attacked the fiery flames consuming the drapes. Savannah felt her throat tighten. Her arms grew weak, but she didn't stop until the fire was out.

Then she reached past the charred drapes and opened her window. She took a deep breath of cold night air into her aching lungs. Then she moved back so Victoria could have a turn.

Savannah sank down onto the edge of her bed. She watched the lingering smoke escape into the night.

Who did this? a voice inside her mind demanded. Who did this? Why? If I hadn't woken up . . . I would have died!

Victoria turned away from the window. "What more must happen, Savannah, before you will believe me? One of us will die here!"

Savannah rose from the bed. "I have to find Tyler."

"He won't help you!" Victoria cried.

Ignoring her sister, Savannah staggered into the hallway. Tyler! she thought. I have to find Tyler.

She stumbled down the stairs. Tyler met her at the foot of the staircase. "Savannah! What happened?"

She staggered into his arms. "Someone set the drapes in my room on fire," she whispered. Her throat felt raw. "Oh, Tyler, I think someone is trying to kill me."

Tyler's arms tightened around her. "Why would anyone want to harm you?"

Savannah leaned back until she could gaze into his blue eyes. "I don't know, Tyler, but I'm terrified. Someone may have tried to poison me—and now this!"

He touched her cheek. "I don't know how to make you feel safe, except—"

"Except what?" she asked. "Send me back to Whispering Oaks?"

"No, I would never send you back to Whispering Oaks," he said. "But I want you to feel safe. I think we should marry as soon as possible."

Savannah's heart pounded. He is right, she realized. We will be so much closer once we are married. And we'll be stronger together.

"I'll send Hattie to town to purchase lace for my bridal veil."

Tyler kissed her. "You should go back to sleep," he said.

She nodded and trudged back up the stairs. Everything will be all right when Tyler and I are married, she told herself.

Savannah heard footsteps running toward her. "Are you all right?" Lucy asked. "I heard what happened."

"I'm fine. I'm just tired," Savannah said. Lucy followed her back up the stairs.

"What color was the fire?" Lucy asked, her eyes bright.

Savannah sighed. Colors. Lucy loves colors. "I think it was red and orange."

"I would have loved to see it," Lucy admitted.

Savannah entered her room and came to an abrupt halt. Mrs. Mooreland was there—taking down the burned drapes.

Lucy tugged on Savannah's hand. Savannah looked down at her.

"I want to share a secret with you," Lucy said in a whisper.

Savannah shook her head. "Lucy, I'm so tired—"

"It's important," Lucy insisted. "Very important."

Lucy dropped Savannah's hand and darted across the room. She climbed onto the bed and patted the spot next to her. "Come sit here."

I probably won't be able to go back to sleep anyway, Savannah thought. She crawled on the bed next to Lucy. "All right. Tell me a secret."

Lucy's eyes widened and her voice dropped. "Have you ever noticed that the letters of the name Fier can be rearranged to spell f-i-r-e?"

Savannah felt the hair on the back of her neck prickle. "No," she admitted hesitantly. "I have never thought about it."

"You should think about it," Lucy said. "There is an old prophesy that says fire will destroy the Fiers. My own parents died in a horrible fire, part of the Fier curse."

Savannah swallowed hard. A fire? Her parents died in a fire? Is that why Lucy is fascinated with fire? she wondered.

Lucy scrambled off the bed. "When it began, it was small, with red and yellow flames," she said in a raspy voice. "But then it started to grow." She swept her hands through the air, forming a wide circle.

"It grew and grew"—she pressed her hands together and moved them toward the ceiling. Then she spread them apart—"until it became big and powerful. And beautiful. With all the colors of a rainbow and more."

Lucy waltzed across the room. "The fire roared like thunder. And the man and woman inside began to dance. They danced in the flames."

Lucy stood on tiptoe. "The flames were so beautiful. Red. Orange. And blue. They swirled around. And when the woman screamed, they swirled faster and faster."

Lucy began to spin around, laughing and laughing. "The flames got brighter and hotter until they were everywhere. Dancing around my mother and father."

Savannah stared in stunned horror at Lucy. *Why is she laughing? Why does she sound so excited? She's describing the fire that killed her parents!*

Chapter
23

Savannah climbed off the bed. "Lucy, you don't have to tell me any more."

Lucy stumbled to a halt, breathing hard, her cheeks bright red, a frightening, wild-eyed look on her face. "The flames got hotter. My mother screamed!"

Savannah wrapped her arms around Lucy. "It's all right, Lucy," Savannah said quietly. "It was long ago and it's over now."

Lucy wrenched free. "They kept dancing. They kept dancing without me!"

Lucy ran from the room. Savannah started to go after her.

"Leave her alone," Mrs. Mooreland said harshly.

Startled, Savannah spun around. She had forgotten that Mrs. Mooreland was in the room.

"She's upset," Savannah protested. "She needs—"

"She needs to be left alone," Mrs. Mooreland

snapped. "Lucy is right about the prophesy. But she didn't tell you everything. Lucy—"

Mrs. Mooreland stopped speaking and stiffened, her eyes focused on something behind Savannah.

Savannah turned and saw Tyler standing in the doorway. "I forgot to ask if you would like to change rooms," he said. "Will the smell of the smoke bother you?"

"No," Savannah assured him, "I opened the window. I think most of the smoke is gone now."

Tyler gave her a short nod. Then his gaze slid past Savannah and settled on Mrs. Mooreland. "Savannah and I are moving up the wedding date."

Two mornings later, Savannah unpacked the wedding gown she had brought all the way from Whispering Oaks. Her mother's wedding gown.

She showed it to Hattie so the young maid could find matching lace for a veil. When Hattie left, Savannah ran her hand over the white silk and sighed.

Maybe Tyler is right. Maybe things will change once we are married. Victoria will realize that no matter what she says or does, we will not return to Whispering Oaks. And Mrs. Mooreland and Lucy will have to accept the fact that I never plan to leave Blackrose Manor.

Savannah lifted her gaze to the charred window frame. After hearing the excitement in Lucy's voice when she described the fire that killed her parents, Savannah suspected the girl had set fire to the drapes.

A horse screamed in terror.

Savannah ran to the open window. "Whisper!" she cried. The big black horse bucked and reared

"No," Savannah whispered. Hattie was in the saddle, clinging to Whisper's mane.

She can't control him, Savannah thought. She's going to fall.

Savannah started for the door. She heard Whisper scream again. Then she heard a dull *thud*.

Chapter
24

"No! No! No!" Savannah cried as she ran down the stairs. She dashed out the front door.

Hattie lay on the ground, her right leg twisted at an unnatural angle. Savannah could hear her moaning.

Whisper pranced around her, tossing his head.

I have to get him away from Hattie. "Easy, Whisper," Savannah crooned as she edged toward the horse.

She could see the whites of his eyes. He's terrified, she thought.

Savannah took a step closer. Whisper reared up. His hooves above Hattie's head.

"I can't move," Hattie screamed.

Whisper plunged down. Savannah heard a horrible crunching sound when his hooves met the bones in Hattie's skull.

"Hattie," Savannah shrieked. She rushed over to the girl. Whisper bolted.

"Oh, Hattie." Savannah knelt down beside the girl. Her forehead was smashed in. Savannah could see pieces of brain tissue mixed with the blood.

Savannah heard the sound of approaching footsteps. She twisted around. Mrs. Mooreland strode up to her. The housekeeper pressed her lips tightly together at the sight of Hattie's broken body.

"This is my fault," Mrs. Mooreland whispered hoarsely. "Hattie told me she had to go into town. I told her to take a horse. I never dreamed she would take yours."

Savannah shook her head. "It's not your fault," she said. "May I have your apron?" she asked quietly.

Mrs. Mooreland didn't hesitate. She untied her black apron and handed it to Savannah. Savannah gently covered Hattie's youthful face.

Victoria ran up to them, her cheeks burning a bright red. She gazed around wildly. Then she reached down and grabbed Savannah's arm, dragging her to her feet.

"The evil forces are growing stronger," Victoria cried. "I can no longer hold them back. We must leave. We must leave now!"

Savannah put a comforting arm around Victoria's shoulder, trying to calm her. "This was an accident. A horrible accident—"

"No! This happened because of the curse! The curse did this! I told you bad luck followed Tyler's family." Victoria grabbed Savannah's arms and shook her. "We must leave."

Savannah felt sick with sorrow. Victoria is insane, she realized. She truly is.

Victoria shook Savannah again.

"Yes, Victoria," Savannah said quietly. "We'll leave tonight. You should go back to bed now and take a nap so you will be rested for our journey."

Savannah hated to lie to her sister. But it was the only way to calm her, and Savannah needed time to decide what to do.

"Come with me," Victoria begged.

"I can't—"

"I'll see to Hattie," Mrs. Mooreland interrupted.

Savannah never expected such understanding from the housekeeper. "Thank you," she said.

Mrs. Mooreland nodded. "Your sister is right. You must break your engagement to Tyler and leave Blackrose Manor—before it is too late."

I can't deal with Mrs. Mooreland now, Savannah thought. I'll have a long talk with her later—after Victoria is asleep.

"Please find Tyler and tell him what happened," Savannah instructed Mrs. Mooreland. Then she led Victoria to her room.

"The evil is near," Victoria whispered as she crawled into bed.

Savannah drew the blankets over her sister. "You'll be safe here," Savannah assured her.

Victoria handed Savannah her black pouch. "Sprinkle the dirt from Mother's and Father's graves around the bed," Victoria said. "It will keep the evil away while I sleep."

Savannah reached into the pouch. Victoria grabbed

her hand. "Be sure and save some for yourself. You'll need to be rested for our journey tonight."

Savannah fought back her tears. I can't let Victoria see how upset I am, she thought. "I'll save some," she promised.

She sprinkled the dirt around the bed and quietly left the room.

Savannah wandered over the grounds of Blackrose Manor, her mind crowded with thoughts of Hattie and Victoria. She wanted to talk with Tyler, but he was taking care of Hattie's body.

As hard as Savannah tried, she could not convince herself that Hattie's death was an accident.

I am certain that I was the one who was supposed to die this morning. A cold shiver traveled through her body. Whisper is my horse.

Savannah rubbed her hands up and down her arms, but she didn't feel any warmer.

In her mind Savannah could still hear the horse's terrified screams, see it rearing up in fear.

She knew there were herbs that could make an animal go mad. Even something as simple as a burr under Whisper's saddle could have made him act so wild.

What about the dark arts? Could Victoria have done something to Whisper?

Savannah believed Victoria would do almost anything to leave Blackrose Manor. Perhaps she thought she could frighten me into running away. She can't have planned to kill me, Savannah thought.

She pressed her hands against her throbbing temples. I don't want to think about the horrible things that have happened. I don't want to think about anything.

She began walking faster and faster. She walked until her legs and feet ached. She walked until she was exhausted, too tired to think.

When the sun began to set, Savannah returned to the manor. It was cold and dark inside. And so quiet.

I should look in on Calico, Savannah thought. Hattie would want me to take care of him. She hurried into the kitchen and checked the wood box. Empty.

"Calico!" she called softly. She glanced around the dark kitchen, but could see no sign of the cat.

As she turned to leave, she heard a noise. Holding her breath, Savannah listened intently.

The sound was from close by—a cat's contented purring.

"Calico?" she called again. She lit a candle and knelt on the floor. In the dim light she could see dark red liquid in a large puddle on the floor. It must have dripped from the oven, Savannah realized. She leaned closer.

Blood, she thought. It's blood. Calico crouched next to the puddle—greedily lapping up every drop.

Chapter 25

Savannah stifled a cry and covered her nose with her hand. She could smell it now. She could smell the rusty odor of blood.

Why did blood drip out of the oven? she wondered with increasing dread. *Why?*

Her heart thudded painfully against her chest. Savannah reached out and wrapped her quaking fingers around the cold iron handle of the oven door. She jerked the door open.

"Mrs. Mooreland!" Savannah shrieked, fear knotting her throat.

The housekeeper had been stuffed inside the large oven. Her eyes were dry and staring. Her pale face frozen in a horrified grimace.

Her right hand was holding her throat. Her left arm was dangling over her head, the blood covering her wrist.

Someone cut off her hand! Savannah realized. She could see the white bone. See the veins and clumps of muscle.

Savannah scrambled to her feet and stumbled back. Her candle wavered.

Then she noticed the strange markings drawn on the floor. Drawn with blood.

What do they mean? Savannah wondered. And then she shuddered as she remembered Victoria using chicken feet to scrawl messages in blood.

Did she use Mrs. Mooreland's hand to make these marks?

"Dark magic!" Savannah whispered hoarsely. "Dark magic was involved in Mrs. Mooreland's death!"

I must find Victoria. I must find Victoria now!

She ran out of the kitchen and headed for the stairs. She stopped when she heard voices. Harsh, angry voices.

She stopped and listened.

The shouting grew louder.

She followed the sounds until she reached the music room. Then she opened the door and peered inside.

Tyler was laughing, laughing even though Victoria held a knife on him.

"What do you think Savannah would say if she knew you put the poison in her sausage, and set her curtains on fire, and fed jimsonweed to her horse? Do you think she would still be so loyal to you then?" Tyler said.

Victoria took a menacing step forward. "She would understand. I would make her understand that I was trying to protect her, trying to get her away from this place. And I will make her understand why you must die!"

Victoria raised the large knife. The steel glinted in the candlelight.

"No!" Savannah cried. She dropped her candle onto the stone floor and charged into the room. She hurled herself at Victoria.

Savannah and Victoria hit the hard stone floor with an echoing thud. Savannah tried to wrench the knife away from her sister.

Victoria shrieked and rolled over until she was on top of Savannah. Her eyes were bulging, her face contorted with rage. "Do not try to stop me!" she screamed. "I must end the curse!"

Victoria rolled to the side, trying to break away from Savannah.

Savannah fought to hold on to her sister. She grabbed Victoria's hair with both hands.

With all her strength, Savannah jerked Victoria back.

Victoria cried out. She collapsed next to Savannah.

Savannah released her hold on Victoria's hair. "I didn't want to hurt you, Victoria, but I couldn't let you murder Tyler."

Victoria opened her mouth to speak, but only a guttural sound escaped her throat. Tears welled in her brown eyes and spilled onto her cheeks.

Then Savannah saw the pool of blood spreading across the stone floor. "You're hurt!" she cried.

Savannah pulled her sister close and cradled Victoria in her arms. She could feel Victoria's warm blood soaking through her dress.

"What happened?" Savannah murmured. Then she saw the knife sticking out of Victoria's side. Victoria rolled onto her own knife.

Victoria fought to draw air into her lungs. She wrapped her cold, trembling fingers around Savannah's hand. "You don't know what you have done," Victoria said in a weak voice.

Tears filled Savannah's eyes. "I have killed you," she whispered. "Oh, Victoria. I am so, so sorry. I didn't mean to. I didn't mean to kill you."

"Worse," Victoria rasped. "You have let the evil live. Be careful. You must be very careful. I . . . I love you, Sissy."

Victoria gave a choking sound. Then bright red blood bubbled between her lips.

Chapter
26

Victoria took one last rattled breath. Her eyes fluttered closed.

"Nooooooo!" Savannah wailed in anguish. "Not my sister. Not my dear sister. Please!" She shook Victoria. "Victoria, wake up. Wake up! I will take you home to Whispering Oaks. You don't have to stay at Blackrose Manor. I will take you back to Whispering Oaks!"

Savannah touched Victoria's pale cheek. Already her skin was growing cold. And it would grow colder.

"Oh, Victoria! I have killed you!" Savannah cried through her sobs.

Savannah stiffened when strong hands grabbed her shoulders and pulled her to her feet. Away from Victoria's body.

Tyler. Savannah looked up into his blue eyes. "Oh,

Tyler," she whispered in a voice thick with grief. "What have I done?"

He wrapped his arms around her and pressed her cheek against his shoulder. "You have saved my life," he said quietly. "She was determined to kill me—one way or another. You had no choice."

"But it hurts. It hurts so much."

He ran his hand along her back soothingly. "I know, love, but it is for the best. The woman you killed was not your sister."

Savannah jerked her head back.

"This girl was not the Victoria I met at Whispering Oaks," he said softly. "This girl was quite mad. You heard what she said, Savannah. She tried to kill you too. She would never have done that if she were sane."

Savannah squeezed her eyes tightly shut. He's right, she thought. She felt so sad. So empty.

I have to tell Tyler what happened to the housekeeper, Savannah suddenly thought. "I think Victoria killed Mrs. Mooreland—" she began.

"Mrs. Mooreland?" Tyler interrupted.

Savannah opened her eyes. "I found her body stuffed in the oven—mutilated."

"Mutilated?" he repeated in a shocked voice.

"Victoria practiced the dark arts," Savannah admitted reluctantly.

She felt Tyler shudder as he held her. "Poor Mrs. Mooreland," Tyler said. "I can't believe she is dead."

Savannah began to shake uncontrollably. So much sadness surrounds us, she thought. Sadness and death. "Oh, Tyler, whatever will we do now?" she asked.

She heard him swallow hard. Then he took a deep breath. "As harsh as it sounds, we must go on with our lives."

He cradled her face between his strong hands. "I know you will mourn your sister's death—but I want you to marry me now."

Savannah stared at him. "Now?"

He hesitated, gazing at her intently. "After Victoria has been laid to rest."

I am so tired of being unhappy, Savannah thought. I want this. I want to be happy. I think I could be happy with Tyler.

Savannah nodded.

Tyler kissed her hands. "You won't regret it."

The cold wind whipped Savannah's cloak around her as she stood beside her sister's coffin. Savannah wore Victoria's black pouch pinned to her skirt. It had not protected Victoria from the evil, but it was all Savannah had left of her sister.

Savannah stared down at the deep hole the men had dug. She shuddered at the thought of Victoria spending eternity in that hole.

"I wish I could have buried you at Whispering Oaks, Victoria," she whispered. "I wish I could have buried you beside Mother and Father. But the road is too long, the plantation too far away. You will be happy here. I shall bring flowers to your grave every day. I promise."

Savannah felt Tyler slip his arm around her. She leaned her head against his shoulder.

Maybe the bad times are behind us, she thought.

The war is over. My sister has found release from the insanity that gripped her—and I will never have to worry about Victoria taking another life.

Tyler and I will be together forever.

The men lifted the ropes attached to Victoria's casket. They swung the casket out over the dark hole.

Only happiness awaits me now, Savannah told herself. She tried to will herself to believe it. Only happiness. My wedding is tomorrow. Tomorrow I will become Mrs. Tyler Fier.

Snap!

Savannah jumped.

One of the ropes supporting the casket broke.

The casket fell into the grave.

The lid sprang open.

Savannah saw her sister's corpse.

Victoria's dark eyes were open. Staring accusingly at Savannah.

And the wind howled Victoria's words of warning—*If we go to Blackrose Manor, one of us will be buried there before the year is out!*

Chapter
27

The following day Savannah walked down the narrow aisle of the small stone church.

No organ music played. No guests had gathered. Savannah did not wear white lace.

She wore the black of mourning.

Her eyes were puffy and swollen. The sight of Victoria staring at her accusingly had kept her awake and crying all night.

Dressed in a black suit, Tyler stood in front of the minister. His expression was solemn.

Lucy stood beside him, holding a bouquet of black roses. Lucy's lips were set in a grim line.

This should be the happiest day of my life, Savannah realized as she neared the altar.

But how can it be? My Victoria is dead.

Tyler stepped forward and took her hand. She found comfort in the warmth of his grip.

"Today we begin anew," he said quietly, his blue eyes holding hers. "We have been plagued with misfortune from the beginning. Our marriage will bring us the happiness we both want." He gave her a small smile. "Trust me, Savannah."

"I do," she whispered. "I always have."

The minister began to read a passage of scripture in a slow, solemn voice.

Savannah found her thoughts drifting back to the days before the war. She had been happy then. She had been surrounded by a loving family and so many friends.

If only I had married Tyler before the war, she thought. It might have been the marriage I always dreamed of—

White lace.

Magnolias filling the church.

Victoria holding my bouquet. Victoria whole and sane and happy for me.

Zachariah standing beside my future husband.

My father leading me up the aisle, his strong arm offering support.

My mother happily weeping as she sat in the front pew.

But I waited.

And now I have nothing but an empty church. And the day that should have been so happy is filled with sadness.

I have lost my entire family, Savannah thought.

Then Tyler's deep voice broke into her memories.

"I, Tyler Fier, take thee, Savannah Gentry . . ."

Savannah lifted her gaze to Tyler's handsome face. He is my family now, she reminded herself.

She glanced down as Tyler slipped a plain gold wedding ring onto her finger. *After all this time, I am truly his wife—until death do us part.*

Savannah repeated her own vows and slipped her token of love onto his finger—a matching gold wedding ring.

"Forever, Savannah," he said in a low voice just before he sealed the vow with a kiss.

"Forever," she repeated when the kiss ended. "Forever."

Savannah and Tyler turned and started back down the aisle.

"We are really and truly sisters now," Savannah said when Lucy approached her.

Lucy reached up and placed her cold hands around Savannah's neck.

Savannah shivered. She hugged Lucy, then stepped back. Lucy tightened her hold. *I can't breathe,* Savannah thought in a panic. She clamped her hands on Lucy's waist and tried to push Lucy away.

But Lucy wouldn't let go. She stood on tiptoe so she could whisper in Savannah's ear.

"Promise me, promise me you won't have children," Lucy begged. "If you do, they will all suffer the curse of the Fiers—as I have suffered. Promise, Savannah. Remember, my parents died in a fire and left me all alone. The same curse is on you now."

Chapter
28

Tyler helped Savannah out of the buggy. He kissed her lightly. "Welcome home, Mrs. Fier."

The sound of Savannah's new name startled her. She smiled uncertainly. "It's hard to believe that we are finally married."

"I know," Tyler agreed as they walked up the stone steps with Lucy trailing behind them. "It's been so long since Zachariah brought me to Whispering Oaks."

Tyler held the door open for Savannah and Lucy. "It's time for you to go to bed, Lucy," Tyler announced as he shut the door behind them. "It's been a long day. I'm sure you're exhausted."

Lucy narrowed her eyes. "Savannah isn't going to bed now. I want to stay up and celebrate with you."

Tyler cupped Lucy's cheek. "Savannah is my wife. I want to spend some time alone with her."

Lucy stomped her foot. "You think I am a child."

"Lucy—" Tyler began.

"I am not a child. I don't have to do what you say," Lucy said, bracing her hands on her hips.

Nothing is as it should be today, Savannah thought. I can't even be alone with my own husband.

"As long as you live here, you will do exactly as I say," Tyler warned Lucy.

"I hate you!" she cried shrilly. She raced up to the second floor, Tyler right behind her.

Savannah lifted her skirts and rushed after them. She caught Tyler's arm. He stopped and looked at her.

"Let her go. You were right. It has been a long day. She will fall asleep on her own," Savannah told him.

They heard a high-pitched scream, a crash, and then another scream. Tyler grabbed Savannah's hand and they hurried into Lucy's room.

Lucy picked up one of her precious dolls and threw it at Tyler. He caught it easily.

"I am not a child!" Lucy cried. "You bring me all these stupid dolls because you think I am a child. You never noticed that I grew up."

She tore the head from one of the dolls and threw it at Savannah. It landed near Savannah's feet and stared up at her with unblinking eyes. Just like Victoria in her coffin, Savannah thought.

"Lucy," Tyler warned in a low, threatening voice. "Stop now."

"No! I can do anything I want. I'll kill them! I'll kill them all!"

What is wrong with her? Savannah thought. Why is she acting this way?

"You could have married me, Tyler. You could have

married me. Then I could stay up and talk to you. Then you wouldn't tell me to go to bed." Lucy ripped the arms off another doll. Cotton stuffing floated through the room.

Victoria was right, Savannah realized. Lucy does want Tyler all to herself. Her feelings are much stronger than a little girl's.

Lucy grabbed another doll and began ripping it apart. Tyler stormed out of the room, a thunderous expression on his face.

Savannah stepped farther into the room. "Lucy," she called out softly. "Lucy, remember, we are sisters now. We can talk."

Lucy spun around and bared her teeth. She curled her fingers into claws. "I don't want to be your sister anymore. Your sister died. You killed her. I don't want you to kill me."

Savannah gasped. She backed away from Lucy. Does she really think I would hurt her?

Savannah felt relieved when Tyler burst back into the room. "You are right, Lucy," he said in a low, calm voice. "I failed to notice that you had grown up. You are too big for dolls now."

Breathing heavily, Lucy sank down onto her bed. "I'm not a child."

Cautiously, Tyler stepped closer. "No, you are not a child. I would not give this to a child."

Savannah watched as Tyler opened his hand. A ruby ring was cradled in his palm. "This belonged to my mother. She told me to give it to you when you grew up," Tyler told Lucy.

Lucy uttered a cry of surprise. "It's beautiful, Tyler."

"So are you," Tyler said. He took Lucy's hand and slipped the ring onto her finger. Lucy held up her hand and admired the sparkling jewel.

"I am all grown-up now, aren't I?" she asked.

"Yes, you are," Tyler said.

With a triumphant smile, Tyler looked over Lucy's head at Savannah. Relieved that Lucy was calm at last, Savannah returned his smile.

But that night she couldn't stop thinking about Lucy. Savannah took a deep breath and told Tyler everything Lucy had said to her at the church.

Tyler's expression grew somber.

A cold chill ran along Savannah's spine. A feeling of heavy dread filled her.

Tyler walked to the window and drew the black drapes back. He gazed out at the darkness in silence.

"I hoped I would never have to tell you this," he said finally. Tyler turned and met Savannah's gaze.

"Lucy killed her parents."

Chapter
29

Savannah heard something shatter. Only then did she realize she had dropped her wineglass. The wine pooled on the floor like blood.

The room tilted and swirled around Savannah. She gasped for air.

Lucy killed her parents! Lucy killed her parents!

The words echoed through her mind like a wailing wind.

She staggered back and fell into a chair.

"What are we going to do?" she asked.

"Lucy will have to be taken away. After the way she acted tonight . . . I think you could be in danger."

Tyler stood, walked to the fireplace, and gazed into the fire burning in the hearth. "I thought I could take care of her, but I can't. It is too risky to have her at the house," Tyler said somberly.

Savannah rose and walked over to Tyler. She rested

her hand on his back. "You're right. We have to do what is best for Lucy and ourselves."

"I don't want you to say anything to Lucy about my decision," he said quietly. "Once I have made arrangements for Lucy to live elsewhere, I will explain the situation to her."

He turned from the fire. He appeared worried and exhausted. "I don't want Lucy to think you had anything to do with my decision."

He took Savannah's hands and squeezed them. "I don't want Lucy to be angry with you," he said in a ragged voice. "I don't want you to die next."

Chapter
30
———

A few nights later Savannah sat at the dressing table in her room, getting ready for bed. She slowly ran her brush through her blond hair.

She had not seen Lucy since the night they returned from the wedding. Lucy claimed she was unwell and needed to rest.

I miss Victoria, Savannah thought. Each morning she walked to Victoria's grave and placed fresh roses next to her sister's headstone.

She couldn't stop thinking about the horrible fight with her sister. Over and over again she saw the madness in Victoria's eyes, the glint of the sharp knife.

There is nothing else you could have done, she assured herself for the hundredth time. Victoria was about to kill Tyler.

Savannah leaned over and blew out the candle. Shadows swallowed the room. The only light came from the small fire in the hearth.

She rose from the chair and strolled over to the window. The garden was black. So black.

As she turned from the window, a flash of light caught her eye. She peered down and saw a torch moving around on the grounds. Tyler must be taking a late walk, she thought.

Savannah understood his restlessness. He had so much on his mind these days. He would be sending Lucy away soon, and Savannah knew that troubled him.

I hope he doesn't stay out too long, Savannah thought. She padded across the cold stone floor and slipped beneath the quilts on her bed. She snuggled down deeper and closed her eyes. But sleep would not come.

I wish I could think of a way to help Tyler, Savannah thought. She rolled over onto her side.

What was that? Savannah sat up. She thought she heard the door slam downstairs. It must be Tyler, she thought. She slid out of bed and crept to the window. She could no longer see the torch.

She heard another sound and froze.

The sound of tiny footsteps.

Running.

Running across stone.

Lucy?

Bang! Savannah's door flew open.

Lucy stood on the threshold, breathing heavily, her cheeks a fiery red.

The flames from the hearth were reflected in her glittering black eyes.

She stared at Savannah.

And then she began to laugh hysterically.

"I know the truth!" she called out in a singsong voice. "I know the truth!"

Chapter
31

Lucy spun around and dashed out the door.

Oh, no! Savannah thought. Lucy knows she is being sent away from Blackrose Manor.

Lucy liked to hide in the shadows. Lucy liked to learn secrets.

Tyler! I must warn Tyler. Who knows what Lucy will try to do to him!

Savannah rushed across the room to the dressing table and grabbed a candle. She lit it in the fireplace and hurried out of the room. Where could Lucy have gone? I must find Tyler first, she decided. Then we can both worry about finding Lucy.

Savannah walked down the hallway until she reached the stairs. The stone felt freezing against her bare feet. Savannah shivered.

I must find Tyler. Savannah scurried down the

stairs. The candle flame danced wildly—then died. Throwing Savannah into darkness.

She froze. There are candles in the parlor, she told herself. I just have to get down the rest of the stairs and into the parlor.

Savannah stepped down. Her foot landed on the edge of the next step. She tripped. And felt herself falling. Falling headfirst down the hard stone stairs.

Chapter
32

Savannah landed at the bottom of the staircase. In a daze she realized she had fallen on something soft. Something warm.

A body!

Savannah scrambled away from it. She peered through the darkness. Lucy. It's Lucy.

Savannah cautiously reached out and shook the girl gently. "Lucy?"

No answer.

I must find a candle. I must see how badly Lucy is hurt.

Savannah struggled to her feet and made her way to the parlor. The fire in the hearth crackled and popped.

She found the small stub of a candle on a nearby table and quickly lit it.

Her blood thrummed through her temples as she hurried back to Lucy. Her knees quivered.

Savannah gasped as the light from her candle fell on Lucy's crumpled body. Lucy's arms were pinned beneath her. A circle of blood surrounded her.

And her face . . . her face was smashed in. Just like her porcelain doll's.

Savannah's stomach lurched. I must find Tyler and tell him what happened. The garden. He was in the garden. She rushed outside.

"Tyler!" she called into the darkness.

Only the howling wind answered. It blew her candle out.

Savannah shuddered. "Tyler!" she shouted again. Then she saw pale yellow light escaping from beneath a door at the far end of the mansion.

Where does that door lead? she wondered. She ran over and tried the latch. Unlocked. She slowly pulled the door open and slipped inside.

She found a stairwell lit with huge torches. These stairs must lead to the cellar, Savannah thought. She headed down.

When she reached the bottom of the stairs, she saw a man hunched over a table. A vial of steaming liquid bubbling beside him.

"Tyler!" Savannah gasped.

He spun around quickly. "Savannah! I wasn't expecting you."

"I had to find you. Lucy is dead!" Savannah cried.

"Yes, I know," he said coldly. He stepped toward her.

Savannah could see more of the table now. It was

covered with vials and jars. Then she saw something that made her scream.

A severed hand—with Lucy's ruby ring on one finger.

"You killed her!" Savannah cried. "You killed Lucy."

"I really had no choice," Tyler replied in a calm voice.

He advanced on Savannah with a grin. "You see, Savannah, I wanted you to be the last one to die!"

Chapter
33

Savannah backed away as Tyler moved toward her one slow step at a time.

"You killed Mrs. Mooreland too, didn't you?" she cried. She remembered Mrs. Mooreland's severed hand.

"Yes," he confessed, his eyes glowing with triumph. "Yes! I killed Mrs. Mooreland. Yes, I killed Lucy! They tried to keep you away from me."

"Victoria was right about you!" Savannah cried. "She knew you were evil. And I killed her. I killed my own sister to protect you."

Savannah felt hatred pump though her body. "How could you do this to me?" she screamed.

"That's not all I did," Tyler told her. "I killed Zachariah too." He held up his scarred palm. "He gave me no choice. We were on opposite sides of the war. He stabbed me with his bayonet."

Savannah shuddered. Zach was trying to warn me when he came to me that night at Whispering Oaks, she realized. He was trying to warn me about Tyler!

"And if you hadn't been on opposite sides of the war?" she demanded. "What then? Would you have killed us all at Whispering Oaks?"

"I told you, Savannah. The war changed us. It changed us all."

He took a big step toward her.

Savannah backed up and slammed against the wall.

A victorious smile spread over Tyler's face. "There is no one to help you, Savannah." He held out his hands. "Only me. Come to me."

"No!" Savannah shouted. She searched the room for a way to escape.

Tyler is blocking the stairs, she thought. I must get him away from the stairs.

And then she noticed a torch burning near her.

Tyler stepped closer.

Savannah held her breath and waited. Just come a little closer, Tyler, she thought. Just a little closer.

Tyler took another step forward.

Savannah grabbed the heavy torch and slammed it down on Tyler's head. Tyler stumbled and fell to the cold stone floor.

Savannah watched in terror as Tyler struggled to get to his feet. He threw his head back and released an angry howl. Then he lunged for her.

She ducked and twisted to the side. Tyler bashed into the wall.

Savannah spotted a pitchfork leaning in the far corner. She scurried across the room, snatched it up, and whirled around.

Tyler leaned against the wall for support. His head hanging down. Savannah raised the pitchfork and started toward him.

"You should have told me Victoria practiced the dark arts," Tyler said, fury filling his voice.

Savannah faltered. He straightened up, his eyes glittering. "You shouldn't ever have kept that secret from me. Victoria almost ruined everything."

Victoria, Savannah thought. Victoria is dead because of you. Savannah rushed at Tyler, the pitchfork raised high. Then she plunged the pitchfork into his chest with all her strength.

She felt the metal prongs stab deep into his flesh. Heard his ribs crunch.

Tyler stood his ground. He did not stagger back. He did not howl in pain. He did not bleed.

He wrapped his hands tightly around the handle of the pitchfork and jerked the prongs out of his chest.

This can't be happening, Savannah thought. It can't be.

Tyler laughed maniacally. "You can't kill me, Savannah! I died at Gettysburg!"

Chapter
34

"Yes, Savannah, I died. Your brother killed me. He stabbed me in the gut. Do you know how painful it is to die from a gut wound, Savannah? The pain is unbearable. And it takes a long time to die."

He's *dead*. Savannah was stunned. She couldn't move. She could hardly think.

"It gave me time to plan," Tyler said. "And to realize that my love for you is undying. Didn't we say forever? Isn't that what we promised?"

They slowly began to circle each other. "I found a way to return to you, Savannah," Tyler said. "I found a way for us to be together forever."

Savannah stared at him. She felt the anger and hatred building up inside her.

"Victoria was not the only one who practiced the dark arts," Tyler told her. "But she was a novice. I am a master."

Savannah gasped as the truth hit her. "The two of you were arguing that day because she had learned the truth."

"Yes," Tyler replied calmly. "She found Mrs. Mooreland before you did. She recognized the markings I made in blood on the floor. She knew I was one of the living dead."

"And she knew how to destroy you," Savannah said.

"No. I was never in any danger. As I said, she was a novice. I would have preferred to kill her myself." He shrugged. "But it was almost as entertaining watching you do it for me."

Savannah felt her heart clench. Victoria's dying words screamed through her mind. *You have let the evil live!* What can I do? Savannah thought. What can I do to stop him?

"There is nothing you can do," Tyler said as though he read her mind. "There is an old saying in my family—*Dominatio per malum.* It means 'power through evil.' I have more power than you can imagine, Savannah."

"What do you want from me?" she shrieked. "Why are you doing this?"

"I promised that one day you would regret choosing the South over me. Today is that day."

He leapt toward her. Savannah darted away.

He laughed. "We can play this game all night. Sooner or later you will tire. And then I will win—because I never tire."

Tyler lunged forward. Savannah jumped back and rammed into the table.

"Nooooo!" Tyler cried. He dove for the table, reaching for the bubbling liquid.

Too late. The vial broke, spilling the steaming liquid on Lucy's hand.

The hand jerked as though suddenly alive. The fingers wiggled. Then they went limp. Tyler shrieked in agony.

Chapter
35

"**Y**ou have ruined the ceremony!" Tyler shrieked. "I needed the energy. I have not fed since Victoria's funeral."

He gazed at her. Savannah could see the hatred in his eyes.

"Now I have to kill you to survive. And I so wanted to take my time. To kill you slowly."

Savannah turned to run, but she slipped on the wet floor. Tyler grabbed her and locked his hands around her throat.

He is going to kill me, Savannah thought. Just as he killed the others.

Searing pain filled her chest. Her lungs burned with the need for air. Savannah thought she could smell magnolias.

"Whispering Oaks." Her lips formed the words, but no sound came out.

Her arms fell limply to her sides. Her knees buckled. Her tongue began to swell.

I want to go home, she thought as darkness swept around her. I want to go home.

A howl of pain echoed around the room. The scent of magnolias gave way to the stench of decay.

Savannah felt Tyler's strong fingers loosen around her throat. Air! She sucked in a huge breath.

Tyler released his hold on her. Savannah could only stare at him.

Tyler's eyes bulged and rolled back in his head. He gasped for breath, wheezing and choking.

He is dying, Savannah realized. He is truly dying this time.

"Help me," Tyler begged.

"You are beyond help," Savannah whispered hoarsely, tears stinging her eyes. "Just as I am. We are both doomed."

Tyler's body began to rot. His flesh turned black and fell onto the floor in meaty chunks.

Savannah didn't want to watch, but she couldn't look away.

One of Tyler's eyeballs popped out. It rolled across the floor in front of her feet.

In moments all that remained of Tyler were clean white bones.

Blackrose Manor

After that Savannah could feel her heart turn as black as the roses in this garden," the old woman said as she plucked another black rose from a bush. "Now you know the story of poor doomed Savannah, the girl who had everything . . . and lost it all."

She crushed the delicate rose with her gnarled hands. "The girl who killed her own beloved sister." She tossed the crushed petals onto a nearby grave. The headstone read VICTORIA GENTRY.

"Yes, now you know *my* story. My tragic story. Isn't that right, dear?" Savannah turned toward the chair next to hers.

Tyler sat beside her, his skeletal face set in a horrified grin, his wedding ring shining around the white bone of his finger.

About the Author

"Where do you get your ideas?"

That's the question that R. L. Stine is asked most often. "I don't know where my ideas come from," he says. "But I do know that I have a lot more scary stories in my mind that I can't wait to write."

So far, he has written nearly five dozen mysteries and thrillers for young people, all of them bestsellers.

Bob grew up in Columbus, Ohio. Today he lives in an apartment near Central Park in New York City with his wife, Jane, and son, Matt.

The Fear family has many dark secrets. The family curse has touched many lives. Discover the truth about them all in the

FEAR STREET SAGAS

Next . . .
THE SIGN OF FEAR
(Coming mid-November 1996)

The Fear family's ancient amulet is the source of their evil power. Now, read about the very first Fear—and learn the terrifying story of how the amulet was created. . . .

Fieran, a young warrior, belongs to an ancient tribe whose members practice dark magic. Fieran uses his strong will to create an amulet of great power. When the girl he loves betrays him, Fieran is destroyed.

But the evil of the Fear amulet lives on. . . .

Now your younger brothers or sisters can take a walk down Fear Street....

R·L·STINE'S
GHOSTS of FEAR STREET®

1	Hide and Shriek	52941-2/$3.99
2	Who's Been Sleeping In My Grave?	52942-0/$3.99
3	Attack of the Aqua Apes	52943-9/$3.99
4	Nightmare in 3-D	52944-7/$3.99
5	Stay Away From the Treehouse	52945-5/$3.99
6	Eye of the Fortuneteller	52946-3/$3.99
7	Fright Knight	52947-1/$3.99
8	The Ooze	52948-X/$3.99
9	Revenge of the Shadow People	52949-8/$3.99
10	The Bugman Lives	52950-1/$3.99
11	The Boy Who Ate Fear Street	00183-3/$3.99
12	Night of the Werecat	00184-1/$3.99

A MINSTREL® BOOK

FEAR STREET® SAGA

Collector's Edition

Including
The Betrayal
The Secret
The Burning

R·L·STINE

Why do so many terrifying things happen on Fear Street? Discover the answer in this special collector's edition of the *Fear Street Saga* trilogy, something no Fear Street fan should be without.

Special bonus: the Fear Street family tree, featuring all those who lived—and died—under the curse of the Fears.

Coming in mid-October 1996

From Archway Paperbacks
Published by Pocket Books

POCKET BOOKS

It's a new school year! And it's time for Fear!

Presents The

1997 Calendar

A sixteen month calendar that starts in September. When your new year really begins! It's a year and a half of horror! Your favorite Fear Street guys and ghouls are back to send you screaming through the school year with sixteen months of ghostly, gruesome fun!

Plus a special bonus ... A poster of every single Fear Street cover ever made! But be careful — all together they may be more fear than you can handle!

POCKET
B O O K S

Coming soon
from Archway Paperbacks
Published by Pocket Books

1249